DISCARDED BY
URBANA FREE LIBRARY

D0947213

e kept

B

URBANA FREE LIBRARY
(217) 367-4057

M   Hilton, John Buxton.
          The quiet stranger

DATE DUE		
OCT 2 7 1997		
MAY 2 6 2001		
AUG 0 5 2011		
12-9-13		

© THE BAKER & TAYLOR CO.

The Quiet Stranger

by the same author

Superintendent Kenworthy novels

THE HOBBEMA PROSPECT
CORRIDORS OF GUILT
THE ASKING PRICE
THE SUNSET LAW
THE GREEN FRONTIER
SURRENDER VALUE
PLAYGROUND OF DEATH
THE ANATHEMA STONE
SOME RUN CROOKED
NO BIRDS SANG
HANGMAN'S TIDE
DEATH IN MIDWINTER
DEATH OF AN ALDERMAN

Inspector Brunt novels

MR FRED
DEAD-NETTLE
GAMEKEEPER'S GALLOWS
RESCUE FROM THE ROSE

non-fiction

THE LANGUAGE LABORATORY IN SCHOOL
LANGUAGE TEACHING: A SYSTEMS APPROACH

JOHN BUXTON HILTON

The Quiet Stranger

A Derbyshire mystery

URBANA FREE LIBRARY

St. Martin's Press
New York

THE QUIET STRANGER. Copyright © 1985 by John Buxton Hilton. All rights reserved. Printed in the United States of America. No part of this book may be used or reproduced in any manner whatsoever without written permission except in the case of brief quotations embodied in critical articles or reviews. For information, address St. Martin's Press, 175 Fifth Avenue, New York, N.Y. 10010.

Library of Congress Cataloging in Publication Data

Hilton, John Buxton.
   The quiet stranger.

   I. Title.
PR6058.I5Q5 1985   823'.914   84-22309
ISBN 0-312-66111-8

First published in Great Britain by William Collins Sons & Co. Ltd.

First U.S. Edition

10 9 8 7 6 5 4 3 2 1

Author's Note

For my source material, I have leaned heavily on John Brown's *A Memoir of Robert Blincoe*, published in 1832, and reprinted by *Caliban Books* in 1977. I am well aware that there is academic controversy over the reliability of Blincoe's evidence—but where there is smoke, something must be smouldering, and there is no doubt that things were bad at Litton Mill. Readers interested in finding out more about the 'tramping' system of unemployed craftsmen will find a wealth of information in R. A. Leeson's *Travelling Brothers* (Granada, 1979).

I must also record my happy indebtedness to Oliver Gomersal for much assistance, especially in matters concerning the Derbyshire Poor Law; to Mr David Sorrell, the Head of the Derbyshire Museums Service, and to Mrs Hilary Dennis of his staff, whose great-grandmother was one of Needham's child labourers.

CHAPTER 1

The untidy little man in the corner seat looked depressed. Until this morning, he had thought that he was doing rather well.

His name was Brunt. He was a detective-constable. He was twenty-four. The year was 1872 and the month of May had reneged on what the High Peak had the right to expect of it. Grey rain—not a laggard shower left over from April, but a throw-back to the malevolence of February—was driving horizontally across the deserted market-place, obscuring the shot-tower, skidding up the empty Derby streets. It rattled a rhythmless tattoo against the windows of the all but abandoned office to which Brunt had come, characteristically on a Sunday, to write painstaking reports in his civil service cursive hand, the upstrokes elegant and slender, the downstrokes bold and firm, so that his script seemed to leap stereoscopically off the page.

Through the frosted glass door-panel of the inner office, he could see a cloak and bowler on the hatstand, could hear an occasional fart. Inspector Pickford was also at his desk. Brunt penned a careful passage about an uncleared break-in up at Barmoor Clough. He hoped to deposit it so that Pickford could not read it until he had gone. He was never entirely at his ease when he was in the same room as Pickford.

His J nib scratched on. The patternless rain made it difficult to think. Roughly once every twenty minutes, Pickford delivered a flatulent reminder of his presence. Eventually he bellowed for Brunt.

Pickford was a big man, ex-army, preferred to be called Captain rather than Inspector. He took pride in sartorial immaculacy: this morning the centre of his personality was a silk stock held by a pearl pin. Brunt stood in front of him in round-shouldered bagginess. Pickford made no comment except with his eyes. Brunt associated clothes with warmth, decency and minimal expenditure.

'How long have you been in the High Peak Division, Brunt?'

'Four months, bar a week, sir.'

'Nadin seems satisfied with you.'

And that was something. Sergeant Nadin had presided over the limestone hills ever since the county had established a plain-clothes department.

'Yes—Nadin seems satisfied. You might care to know that I'm not.'

Pickford looked at him as if he wished that he could apply certain punishments that had been filtered out of military law in the earlier half of this liberalizing century.

'In fact I would go as far as to say that I cannot think of anything so unpromising in a detective-constable as the ability to satisfy Sergeant Nadin. Just for the sake of remind-ing me—and possibly also yourself, Brunt—how do you interpret your duties?'

'The maintenance of the Queen's peace, sir,' Brunt said, relieved to recognize safe ground.

'By detecting crime.'

'And, with respect, sir—by deflecting it.'

'That is an attitude that will not get you far in this Force.'

That was the crux of the matter. The day Brunt had reported for duty, Sergeant Nadin had looked him up and down.

'So what do you reckon you have come here to do?' he had asked. 'To be a detective?'

He was as scornful on one side of the argument as Pickford was on the other.

'We have very little crime here, Master Brunt. I prefer to call myself a deflective. That way I do not waste time hanging about court corridors, and Her Majesty's Exchequer is saved the cost of prison gruel. Ideally, the objective of a police force should be to render itself superfluous. I put in irregular appearances here and there, and I pride myself that there is very little naughtiness in my bailiwick.'

He sounded bad-tempered, but there was warmth in his eyes.

'There's a young lady I want you to take a look at tomorrow,' he said some weeks later. 'Amelia Pilkington. I think that you and I are going to have no end of fun with her.'

It was ironical that Captain Pickford, this rainy Sunday morning, should have the dossier in front of him.

'Anyone would think that you and Nadin were simply setting out to enjoy yourselves.'

Amelia Pilkington—some of her aliases were also known to Nadin—made her living by misleading the generosity of wealthy widows and elderly invalids in places like Bournemouth and Bath, often portraying herself in such pitiful straits that a single notable gift would consummate the relationship. In Buxton for the last three weeks she had been the constant companion of Sir William Palfreyman, formerly a master-mind in Her Majesty's India Office.

'We'll have a bit of fun here,' Nadin had repeated. 'We'll stick to her shadow till she's sick of the sight of us. And I'll have a quiet word with Sir William. That way, she'll have to work hard for anything she earns. And we shall have saved her from committing a crime.'

'Nothing whatever has happened for three whole weeks,' Pickford complained.

For three weeks Amelia Pilkington had been pushing Sir William about in an invalid chair, accompanying him to concerts, escorting him on carriage-trips, listening to his deadly reminiscences in ornamental gardens and the Pump Room.

'She has broken no law so far, sir.'

'No—because you and Nadin won't let her. Give her some

rope. Stop warning her off. Tell Nadin I want her under lock and key by this time next week.'

He tapped a tabulated manuscript on which he had been working.

'Crime, Detective-Constable Brunt, culminates in two columns of figures. On the left, a summary of complaints, on the right the tally of retribution and retrievals. All you have retrieved since you left the uniformed branch has been one sheep, one umbrella and one circulating library book.'

Because, Brunt was tempted to add, very little else had been stolen. Jimmy Nadin always seemed to know in advance where wickedness was being contemplated, and he always seemed to happen along (or to send Brunt) in time to persuade the villains of the unworthwhileness of their current efforts.

'Of course, Brunt, if you wish to return to testing shop door-handles on wet nights—'

A fresh spatter shook the window in its frame.

'I'm off now, Brunt. Make me six copies of this chart, and leave them on my desk.'

Which took Brunt the remainder of his day, at the expense of the work he had come here to do. He returned on a late evening train, the depression in his eyes visible to discerning strangers.

CHAPTER 2

The rain was still streaking across the valley when the brakes went on for Duffield. The trackside greenery had faded to the pallor of wood-ash by the time they reached Ambergate. At Matlock Bath it was only by the intensified thundering of the wheels that they could tell whether they were in a tunnel or not.

For the first ten miles, Brunt had still brooded. On the one hand was Pickford, who needed blood, like the fox that eats one hen and leaves two dozen in the run with their necks chewed. On the other hand was Nadin, a benign old eccentric who had in his time foiled criminals in their hundreds. The Division was so law-abiding after a quarter of a century of Nadin that one day someone was going to say that it was over-manned. Sergeant James Nadin was shortly due for retirement; Captain-Inspector Pickford would be going on for as long as could be contemplated. Brunt's mind circulated as if it were being driven by a shaftful of uncoordinated cams. Then he began to study the man in the far window-corner.

'Never lose a chance,' Nadin had taught him—he was supposed to be training Brunt as they went—'of playing against a silent stranger. Learn everything you can from looking at him: his health, his wealth, his job, his joys, his hates. It's against the rules in the first stage to ask him any question. You mustn't speak until you know all you can find out. When you've made up your mind what he's had for his breakfast, and what he's looking forward to for his tea, then you can speak to him. Find out how wrong you've been—and where you went astray. Never lose an opportunity—in any waiting-room, or public park, or train—'

A train: this stranger had been established in his corner when Brunt got in. He was a tall man—Brunt put him in his early sixties—a man who had respected his body, never overeaten, never underslept. He was ramrod straight. Retired military? No: Brunt rejected that, by comparison with Pickford. There was something distinguished about this stranger, but it was difficult to say from what it stemmed. His clothes were sober and ordinary, but nearly new: a complete contrast to Pickford's flamboyance. His eyes had a touch of compassion—but they hardened when he spotted that Brunt was studying him. They were eyes that took an avid interest in everything on which they rested: people on platforms, the destination on a luggage-label. He looked so keenly at humdrum things that Brunt wondered whether he had recently returned from a long stay out of this country.

He was what Pickford would have accepted as *officer class*
(which Brunt emphatically was not). Yet if he had been in
the army, it could even have been as a private soldier. He had
a private's hands, cleanly manicured, but extraordinarily
strong: they had done work, the hands of a craftsman. The
care that he took over them suggested that he kept them in
trim for fine processes. He had a workman's fingers—but his
demeanour was that of a master.

After Bakewell, the stranger's manner changed. He became expectant, one might say even nervous. He brought out
a map, unfolded it on his lap and began to follow the railway
with his forefinger. At the same time, he peered closely out of
the window—though there was by now nothing he could see.
Between him and the dark of night, the pane was streaked
with soot.

Hassop—Great Longstone—Little Longstone—the Monsal Head tunnel. The driver notched the cut-off down and
shut off steam for Monsal Dale. Another few minutes, and
the two men would be parted. Phase Two must start: Brunt
would have to speak.

Monsal Dale had a single platform. Two oil lamps, their
wicks badly trimmed, were producing as much black smoke
as they were yellow light. A porter in streaming oilskins held
up his hand to the guard, who slid a green filter over his
lantern.

The stranger was now tense. His square-cut fingers were
drumming against his map. He seemed uneasy to remain
seated. He was like a man fighting an internal battle—one
that he knew he might not win. As they entered the Cressbrook tunnel, he rose to his feet, gave Brunt a broad view of
his back and gazed outwards as if under a compulsion to
study every variation of the carriage lights as they scudded
over the brickwork.

Brunt knew every inch of the line. They were running
parallel to a rising dale, through two tunnels separated by a

gap of about twenty yards. By daylight, this gap presented on the left a sheer face of rock, on the right a sixty-mile-an-hour glimpse of gorge: Water-cum-Jolly Dale. Here the river had been widened to form a mill-lodge. It was a rugged, Byronic prospect. But to catch sight of it, a traveller had to know that it was coming, had to be waiting for it alert.

And that was how the stranger was waiting, though it was unthinkable that he should see anything on such a night as this. His hand moved to the leather strap, and at a well-judged second, he lowered the window. The tone of their rumbling changed as they passed the gap. A thick billow of smoke entered the compartment, sulphurous and choking. The man turned his head.

'I'm sorry.'

'No harm done.'

The stranger took his seat again, carefully hitching his trousers above his knees.

'You have to see it by daylight,' Brunt said. 'One of the most beautiful of our dales. But there's no public right of way: a mill at either end. They'll let you through for a small toll.'

The stranger's eyes were piercing Brunt's face. Brunt went on talking as if he could not stop himself.

'A hundred years ago there was a peppermint mill at the top end. They used the wild mint from the hillside above. Arkwright built one of his mills at the bottom end. Eventually William Newton, Minstrel of the Peak, took it over. And upstream, a man called Ellis Needham—'

The stranger's jaw muscles tightened.

'Needham built new premises at Litton, brought in child labour from the Poor Law. People say it was a bad place to be. But that's all water over the wheel now. It's not a spot many people know about. It's not on the ordnance map, not in the guidebooks.'

'Forgive me—but did I hear you say just now it was beautiful?'

'I'd recommend it to any visitor.'

'Then God forgive you.'

If God did, it seemed unlikely that the stranger ever would. They had less than a couple of miles to go before Brunt had to change to the local line at Miller's Dale. But the stranger also got out at the junction, went back along the rain-pelted platform to the guard's van. From the third-class waiting-room came an upsurge of march-rhythm hymn-singing. The station was the headquarters of the village Methodists. Jack Simmonds, the ticket inspector, took himself out of the service for five minutes' duty.

Contrary to Midland Railway bye-laws, Brunt lowered himself to the rails to cross to the other platform. But before he started to go over, the stranger approached, now curved under the weight of a strongly-bound chest. That might be the answer to him—a sea-faring man. 'Excuse me. I spoke roughly to you just now. No offence meant.'

'No offence taken,' Brunt said.

'You're a man who must know the neighbourhood. Am I right in saying you're a policeman in mufti—and not much in love with your lot?'

Brunt was stunned by the man's mastery of his own game. 'How can I help you?' he asked.

'I'm heading for Litton village.'

'You'll find no one anxious to turn out a carriage on a night like this. There's a good inn down here.'

'No—I mean to finish my journey tonight. It's beginning to irk me.'

'It's three steep miles to Litton. Under that burden—'

'I'm not minded to set it down again till I'm there. So where would you tell a man to lay his head in Litton village?'

The train they had left was already a red buffer-lamp disappearing up Chee Dale. Jack Simmonds was banging the doors of the Buxton shuttle.

'Go to the Cordwainers' Arms, landlady Annie Barker.

Tell her Tom Brunt sent you.'

Brunt hurried over the tracks. Jack Simmonds held a door for him silently, looking at him with the accusing pity that he had for any man who was not in the waiting-room singing Moody and Sankey.

CHAPTER 3

Brunt found Sergeant Nadin delighted with the weekend's progress. Amelia Pilkington, knowing herself watched, but reluctant to leave the town empty-handed, had been compelled to spend an honest and vigorous Sunday. She had all but broken her back pushing Sir William up to Higher Buxton for Matins in St Anne's. Then he had asked to be promenaded along the Duke's Drive, where the first spots of rain had moved in from the south-west. Sir William demanded her company again at tea-time and talked without let or interval about the Relief of Cawnpore. Sergeant Nadin did not know what trifling sweeteners had prevented her from throwing in the towel; but he was satisfied that none of the usual routines was going to work with Sir William.

Brunt reported Pickford's insistence that the Pilkington woman be brought to book within a week. Jimmy Nadin— who looked rather like an organ-grinder's monkey done up in a suit—was unmoved. He seemed to treat Pickford as a mere myth, and had a remarkable talent for staying out of his way.

Brunt spent Monday morning on an alleged theft from a bedroom in one of the big hydros. It turned out that a dressing-case had been mislaid by its owner. In the afternoon he walked four miles to Earl Sterndale on a report of cattle-rustling. It transpired that the beasts had wandered through a gap that a farmer had walked past five times that week without noticing it. Brunt knew that both his reports would eventually be read by Pickford.

Sir William and Miss Pilkington were beginning to look to people like a martinet father and a dutiful but no longer adoring daughter. They quarrelled audibly in public. On the following Thursday, a laboured communication came through internal channels, and Nadin passed it to Brunt without comment. It appeared to have been written with a soft-wood splinter, dipped into chemically deteriorating ink, and it was signed Jno Judson, PC, who had also appended his number. It was an appeal for assistance in what he described as a curious situation. His address was in Litton village.

'An ideal call,' Nadin said, 'for a young man who wants to see himself making his way.'

Brunt looked at him innocently.

'He doesn't give us the slightest idea what it's about.'

'He wouldn't. Not Judson. He probably doesn't know.'

'But if you or I were to ask for assistance, without specifying—'

'Ah, but this is Jack Judson. It's something for Jack to admit that he needs help. Actually to ask for it, by putting pen to paper—'

'That was a pen he used, was it?'

'This will be something worth looking at,' Nadin said.

Brunt looked at his watch. He knew the railway timetable by heart.

'In that case, perhaps we'd better—'

Nadin uncrossed his legs and crossed them the other way.

'There'll be nothing you can't handle on your own.'

So Brunt trod in spring sunshine the uphill road that the enigmatic stranger had climbed with a trunk on his shoulder. Ashbuds were breaking, a cuckoo was calling down in Tideswell Dale. From Tideswell onwards he got a lift on an oil-chandler's cart—though because of the gradient, he had to get off and walk for at least half the distance.

Tommy Lamp-oil (if he had any other surname, even he had ceased using it) picked up items of news as a summer breeze picks up dandelion seeds. Brunt had met him three or four times and they were naturally drawn to each other, each jockeying for information with his own brand of skill. Tommy took in Litton village once a week, and was on his way there now. He seemed to know more about the reasons for Brunt's journey than Brunt did. But Brunt recognized the pattern. Tommy's method was to appear to know everything, putting people off their guard, so that they often ended up by giving Tommy the very information that he claimed to know already.

'Jimmy Nadin will be up later, I suppose?'

'He might.'

'Rum do. They're saying down in Bakewell that Jack Judson's worried.'

Cattle-market gossip?

'Down at the Workhouse,' Tommy said.

Something carried in by a casual, then?

'In the Infirmary.'

The Workhouse Infirmary was the nearest the 1870s had to a geriatric ward. The senile and the mentally incompetent were protected by a discipline that would not have been inappropriate on a recruits' square.

'They're worried in there,' Tommy said.

'Maybe not without reason,' Brunt said, happy to enhance his own appearance of total knowledge.

'Yet nobody will say who he is, though somebody must know. They don't seem to want to put their tongue to his name.'

'Who?' Brunt asked abruptly.

'The man who came up Sunday night. Walked up from Miller's Dale with a sea-chest on his back. Hasn't said a word to a soul since he got there. And I tell you, they're having nightmares in the Workhouse Infirmary.'

Brunt saw an image: two rows of severe beds in the senile paupers' wing in the forbidding stone barracks, an old man screaming in his sleep because the word had come that a

taciturn gentleman had arrived in a village eight miles away;
a fastidious gentleman with the hands of an artisan; a
stranger who had flung open a train window, letting in the
smoke, to try to peer through a black storm into a limestone
gorge; a man who had lost his temper because Brunt had said
that Water-cum-Jolly Dale was beautiful.

'Who do people think he is, then?'

Brunt knew that he was losing face by thus admitting
ignorance. But as he suspected, Tommy Lamp-oil was in no
better position. He sidestepped the question.

'He's staying at the Cordwainers'. Annie Barker's.'

'Annie will know how to handle him.'

They had come to the lower reaches of the high-lying
village. Tommy pulled up to make the first of his calls. Brunt
went on alone up the street of stone houses. Litton was a
settlement that faced exposure to the elements with defiance,
but with no admission of pleasure. The original reasons for
founding a village here had largely disappeared. The lead ore
for which men had mined had paid so meanly that they had
assaulted the rock-ridden soil with equally ungenerous
smallholdings. Then when the ore had petered away, and
their workings had flooded, they were left with their narrow-
ly parcelled, sterile fields. Some had learned frame-knitting,
for which the thread from Ellis Needham's mill, down in the
valley bottom, had been indispensable. Some had gone to
work down there, a few even rising to be overseers. But
Needham got his labour at rates of pay that made Litton men
better off tearing rocks in the limestone quarries. Some said
that a man's dignity had to be sapped before he would work
for Needham. So Litton village was poor, victimized by
weather, fate and nineteenth-century economics, all three of
which it faced in inarticulate but aggressive unity. Brunt had
never had to attend to a case of any substance in Litton, but
he knew that the Littonites could foil him if they wanted to.
And the chances were that they would want to.

Brunt went straight to Judson's house. He had met Judson

once, when he had had to come here to check the alibi of a man suspected of larcenous wiles at Flagg point-to-point races. What had been most striking about the village constable had been his volubility. He was a stranger here, an *offcomed 'un*, who had arrived from the West Riding thirty years ago, and who seemed to wish to compensate alone for the silence of the Peakrels. He was a very difficult man to interrupt. He did not philosophize, he did not formulate principles, he did not endeavour to instruct. He never gave a straight answer to a simple question. His approach to conversation was almost invariably anecdotal. For PC Judson there was no new event that did not recall some old one. His stories were parables whose meaning it was not given to every man to see. And if the answer was lost on the one who had brought the problem, that was something that Judson simply accepted. It was as if he had one day resolved, once and for ever, to reserve his opinions for those intelligent enough to understand them.

Bluff and noisy-booted, he was frankly abashed that Jimmy Nadin had not come himself in answer to his call. Then he started a tale about a young sheepdog that had been trained at the heels of an older animal, but turned loose too soon to bring a flock down from the brow.

It was not easy to turn such a narrative into a dialogue. Fortunately, Judson had to blow his nose in the middle of a sentence.

'This man who came up from Miller's Dale off the late Sunday train—' Brunt managed to begin.

Judson looked surprised that a youngster should know anything.

'Big fellow,' Brunt said. 'Well-groomed but has a workman's hands. Curiously interested in Needham's mill.'

'Doesn't talk,' Judson added. 'And staying at—'

'The Cordwainers'. Annie Barker's.'

'Yes, well, he has to talk to Annie; a few words here and there, what he'd like for his breakfast, and couldn't something be done about opening one of the windows. I mean to say, when did anyone last want a window opened at the Cordwainers'? There's a tale they tell here about two pedlars who came one time, both on the same day, one from Sheffield and one from Nottingham. They both put up at the Cordwainers'—same wares—only different prices—'

'It isn't exactly a crime not to want to talk over-much,' Brunt said. 'Nor to want a breath of fresh air in one of Annie's bedrooms.'

'I was telling you about these two pedlars.'

'Has there been an actual complaint,' Brunt asked, 'about this man at the Cordwainers'?'

'Well, no—but I'm a worried man, Mr Brunt. I was telling you about these pedlars, oh, it'll be a hundred, a hundred and fifty years ago—They killed him, you know, the one from Nottingham.'

'So you think somebody's going to kill this fellow with the sea-chest?'

'George Ludlam, he's given out to be known as. And when the name Ludlam was spoken, there were folk here who bristled. Some folk. Older folk. It's the older folk who are—what's the word I'm looking for? Disturbed. Aye—disturbed.'

'And in Bakewell Workhouse,' Brunt said. 'In the Infirmary. There are one or two worried there too.'

Judson sat back and looked at him, surprised. Clearly this was news in Litton: till Tommy Lamp-oil had done his round.

'They're having nightmares in Bakewell Workhouse.'

'That'll be Ned Woodward and Joe Moss.'

'Will it?'

'I'm not surprised. I can see it now, Mr Brunt. It's all dropping into place.'

He looked over to see whether things seemed to be dropping into place for Brunt, too.

'Don't you see, Mr Brunt—they were all in it together—

Ned Woodward and Joe Moss, now in the Workhouse. And
Peter Townley, Dick Logan, Harry Lockett and Billy Orgill.
I've been here thirty years, and the Locketts and the Logans
haven't spoken to one another in that time. Not till this
George Ludlam came, on Sunday night. Then on Monday,
Harry Lockett's round at Billy Orgill's having sent his wife
round first to strew a few petals for him, as you might say. I
don't like it, Mr Brunt.'

'And what have they got in common, these Locketts and
Logans?'

'They're all in their seventies. I could feel it, I tell you:
Litton bristled. They all used to work down the mill in the old
days—Woodward and Moss too.'

'I suppose there are ways the news could have been carried
down to the Workhouse?'

'Visiting day, Tuesday. Margery Woodward went down
on the carrier's wagon. They were bad days,' Judson said
ponderously. 'Before you were born, and I was still wandering about Heckmondwike with my breeches' arse out. They
were all young men then, Orgill and Logan and Moss.
Aye—and George Ludlam was with them there, too, that's
my betting. I've heard stories. They were bad days at Litton
Mill.

'It's the 1820s I'm talking about—before any of these
Factory Acts. William Newton's mill down at Cressbrook,
that wasn't so bad. But at Ellis Needham's a mile upstream,
there's no tally of what those kids suffered. They were from
London Poor Law, you know—orphans, waifs, strays,
foundlings. Aye, and a few that were found before they were
lost. Six-, seven- and eight-year-olds, working a sixteen-hour
day on a breakfast of water-porridge. And sometimes it was
midday before they could break off from their spindles to eat
that. Ha'penny a day they'd be offered, to work through their
dinner-hour, and as often as not that was another broken
promise. As for punishments: they were hung up over turning machinery.'

Judson's eyes were bulbous with the need to convince.
Brunt knew that it was basically true. He had heard stories
himself. The prosperity of the nation had been borne on some
narrow shoulders.

'Ellis Needham was bad, and his sons even worse, John in
particular. But the worst of the lot were the overlookers.
Because their jobs depended on getting the work out of the
kids that Needham needed. Children thrashed black and
blue. Tormented too, for the sake of it. An eight-year-old
having to open his mouth for an overseer to spit tobacco-
chewings into it.'

'And some of those overseers still live in the village?'

'Ned Woodward was one. So was Billy Orgill.'

'All older men than Ludlam?'

'That's why I'm worried, Mr Brunt. That's why my mind
keeps turning back to these pedlars.'

'Have you talked to Ludlam?'

'I've caught sight of him. He has a hard look. What you
might call a concentrated look.'

Brunt began to think of the report he would have to
submit—a report that Inspector Pickford would read. No
crime, no complaint, no losses to be retrieved.

Judson suddenly got up, as stealthily as if he thought they
were still under observation from the street. He beckoned
Brunt to the window. The police house was opposite the
Cordwainers' Arms, and George Ludlam had just come out
of the front door. His military carriage was more striking
than ever—a straightness of back that gave him an air of
satisfied superiority. And in that manner he was looking at
the small knot of men who had gathered at the road's edge
some twenty paces below him. They certainly looked older
than him, though that might have been more than partly the
effect of their postures. Their shoulders were rounded. None
had shaved within the last twenty-four hours. Their moleskin clothes, trousers and coats that did not match, had been
put on as they had come to hand—if, that is, they took them

off to sleep. Perhaps they had been talking together before George Ludlam appeared, but the sight of him had produced silence.

Ludlam neither paid attention to them nor ignored them. His eye rested on them, and he gave no sign that they had inspired in him any feeling whatever. One of them stepped into the gutter to allow him to pass. But Ludlam made a detour, swung round them in a wide half-circle, then strode down the hill.

'Going down to look at the mill at last,' Judson said. 'You'll make sure Jimmy Nadin knows about all this?'

Only when Ludlam was well out of earshot did one of the men speak. Then it was a mouth-corner syllable that did not carry to the police-house. They moved towards the Red Lion.

'You'd best go and have a word with Annie,' Judson said. 'She's lost a lot of custom since Ludlam knocked on her door.'

CHAPTER 4

The Cordwainers' Arms was a basic inn—oak settles and benches worn smooth by moleskin and corduroy. It must have looked unchanged for centuries. And if she had been here in the fifteenth, Annie Barker would not have looked greatly different, either. Rotund and wheezing, she was five feet tall and top-heavy. She had the reputation of a virago. This had been her prime defence since, widowed by the crumbling shaft of a one-man mine, she had managed the Arms single-handed. Her carping had now become such a habit that she found it impossible to say a good word in public about anything or anyone. But it was known that in private she had her favourites—and for no reason that he could think of, Brunt seemed to be one of them. All the same, she greeted him with lashing fury.

'Take a good look, Sir Detective—fancy sending that man here.'

She stumped from one room to another of her deserted tavern.

'Not a soul. They've all left me. Gone to the Lion.'

Then she laughed, taking pity on what she deemed his innocence.

'Not to worry. I can do with a rest. That's how it goes in Litton. Men who've been going to one house for years suddenly shift to the other. Only this time I know why. They're all scared out of their stockings. So who are you after, Mr Brunt? George Ludlam, or them?'

'Neither. I've just come to see.'

'And to believe everything Jack Judson tells you? He's what you'd call bothered, isn't he?'

'Uneasy.'

'Does he really think that a gentleman like Mr Ludlam is looking for trouble? With the likes of Billy Orgill and Harry Lockett?'

So Ludlam must have qualified for one of Annie's softer spots, too. She made it sound laughable, the notion that Ludlam might be worried by old men in their seventies, with arthritis, induced spinal curvature, wrecked feet in burst boots, not a grain of intelligence in their eyes.

'Jack Judson's all right in his way. He gives us no trouble. But he doesn't know it all. Least of all does he know a thing about George Ludlam.'

Which meant that Ludlam could not have been silent here, that he must have spoken confidences. Brunt did not risk a question that Annie might resent.

'He's one of the world's good men, that's what I know, Thomas Brunt. So might you be, if you were to try hard. You'll be wanting bread and cheese and your usual small beer?'

She took him into her inner parlour, a room remarkable for

its huge quantity of small, largely worthless ornaments—and for its heat. Annie Barker gave the impression of wearing many layers of clothes, yet she still seemed to need hothouse temperatures. She served him a wedge of bread and cheese two inches thick, with half a large raw onion and a horn-handled knife.

'No—it's not from those old fools that trouble will come.'

'You mean you think there'll be trouble? Has he come here looking for someone?'

'Not anyone he was expecting to find,' she said. 'But that he *has* found.'

'That takes a bit of working out.'

'It's easy enough: Eva Hargreaves.'

'I don't know her.'

'You wouldn't. She's been bed-ridden—well, stuck in the house—ever since you started coming here.'

Annie had poured herself a small tankard of porter and was mulling it with the hot end of the poker. Beads of sweat were forming on Brunt's forehead.

'It was the name Eva that did it. Only it was never as Hargreaves that he knew her. When I said she went lame, and that it was something that had happened at the mill when she was a youngster, then he knew.'

She sat back and looked at Brunt as if she had just given him information that went deeper than words.

'Sweethearts, that's what I reckon. Though they can't have been very old.'

'What is it you're trying to tell me, Annie?'

'That when he came here he'd no thought of finding her. When he knew she was here, it seemed to change his whole nature.'

'Jack Judson says he's a non-talking man. He seems to have told you plenty.'

'A man doesn't have to open his mouth to give things away. You ought to know that in your job.'

Brunt cut himself concentric rings of onion.

'And is Eva Hargreaves a widow?'

'She is.'

'And Annie Barker a matchmaker?'

But she seemed not to like the label. He wished he had not said it.

'So how does this make trouble?' he asked.

'She's in the Bagguleys' hands.'

She looked at him as if that explained everything. Then she frowned, angry at his ignorance.

'You wouldn't know. It was before your time. But don't they pass things on in your line of business? You'd better ask Jimmy Nadin about the Bagguleys.'

'It will save time if I ask you.'

'And you think you'll learn a bit more, perhaps. I never thought Jimmy was as sharp as he might have been over the Bagguleys. But then, he had that big, useless tailor's dummy from Derby on his heels, hadn't he? What was his name? Pickford. Pickford said it was all village gossip.'

'And wasn't it?'

Annie Barker looked as if it was only her natural leaning towards ladylike behaviour that stopped her from spitting on the fire.

'Ask Jimmy,' she said, in a tone that amounted to the same thing. 'Let's say Eva fell on worse than bad times when Harry Hargreaves died. They were devoted, Mr Brunt. I always say they went too far with it. There was nothing for either, outside the other. And she'd this bad leg. It got caught in a driving-belt when she was thirteen or fourteen. Harry did everything for her. When it gets like things were between Eva and Harry, too much is taken away when one of them has to go. I ought to know. Didn't the same happen to me? Now the Bagguleys have moved her in with them.'

'Steady a minute. Who are the Bagguleys?'

'Ben Bagguley—ne'er-do-well.'

Annie had said that about most of the men in Litton at one time or another.

'A man without trade. Apprenticed to a stone-mason, never finished his time. Tried lime-burning, cheese-factoring, bought Starve-Acre with what they made off Nell Merridew—was letting his bottom field and mortgaging the rest before he'd been on the land a twelvemonth.'

'Maybe they don't call it Starve-Acre for nothing.'

'It didn't starve Jesse Vernon. But then, Jesse knew when it wasn't a spending day. Bagguley married a woman from the shadow side of Chelmorton who showed him what it was to need ready money.'

'How did they make a fortune out of Nell Merridew?' Brunt asked.

'By fawning over her when she was taken sick; bowls of bread and milk, noggins of brandy from the Lion. By codding her on she was sicker than she was. By making sure, if you want my opinion, that she got sicker than she need be. Molly Bagguley was there all hours of day, then took to sleeping there nights. It wasn't long after that that the end came. And Nell had had a lot of stuff in her house that wasn't there when her daughter came up from Leicester. The Bagguleys said it was all gifts for services rendered.'

'How old was Nell Merridew?'

'Ninety-seven.'

'That might have some professional men thinking in terms of natural causes.'

'She was wanting to get to a hundred, like her mother and grandma before her.'

'Even suppose there was something in it, it would be a difficult case to bring to court,' Brunt said.

'Not if you take account of Isaac Slack.'

'How old was he when the Bagguleys started looking after him?'

'Still siring his kind on borrowed time. I never did think it was only for sick-nursing that Molly Bagguley started dropping round. And you can't tell me her husband didn't know what was going on.'

'It wasn't a case of disability, then?'

'His only disability was that he couldn't get out any more. Anyway, she carried him in enough drink to make sure he did stay at home.'

'And what did they gain from it?'

'Enough to make it worth while swapping his gin bottle for spirits of salt.'

'If he'd drunk spirits of salt, he'd have died in agony.'

'He did die in agony. They made out he'd taken the wrong bottle down from the shelf.'

'What was a bottle of spirits of salt doing on his shelf?'

'She'd taken it to clean his dirty pans with, that was their tale. Not but what they didn't need it. If you're doubting my word, ask old Dr Collins. He certified acid on Isaac's breath and burns in his mouth.'

'Was there an inquest?'

'Accidental. That's what they found. But ask Jimmy Nadin. Jimmy never believed it was an accident. It was that Pickford of yours who put the stopper on it.'

'And how much are the Bagguleys supposed to have made out of it?'

'She only got him so stupefied with one thing or another that he showed her where he kept his savings.'

'That's known for certain, is it?'

'What's known for certain is that Isaac had sovereigns in his house—and none were found.'

'And now the Bagguleys have got George Ludlam's lady-love under their wing?'

'Their *wing*!'

'Where's Ludlam gone now? Down the dale?'

'You're not to go interfering with him.'

'I haven't all the time in the world.'

'Neither has George Ludlam. Leave him alone, Mr Brunt. He's come here to settle things in his mind.'

Brunt finished his beer. There was a limit to what he was

prepared to discuss with Annie Barker. Annie Barker knew
that, too.

'Now don't you go upsetting that good man, Tom Brunt. If
you do, you'll have me to reckon with.'

This was not the eccentric wrath that was Annie's culti-
vated style. It was a genuine appeal. Brunt nodded, to show
that he had taken it in. But he did not commit himself.

CHAPTER 5

Brunt felt the peace of the dale settle over him, as the grey
walls of the mill that had once been Ellis Needham's fell back
behind him. For a mile ahead the water was placid, almost
motionless, reflecting the greys and greens of the steep flank.
On his right, a bank of pristine sedge stretched almost as far
as the lower mill at Cressbrook. That institution, in the
nascent industrial revolution, had been very different from
the one at the Litton end, an exercise in paternalism. It had
even boasted a Leisure Farm, where the youngsters had had
the freedom of the fields on Sundays.

It was possible that Needham had taken advantage of
Cressbrook's reputation to attract his own labour force. Of
one thing no man was in doubt: life for the infants in
Needham's Apprentices' House had been as near hell as an
uncaring man could devise. That was why George Ludlam
had taken exception when Brunt had called the dale beautiful.

But the beauty was undeniable, and by widening the river
to feed the weirs, man had actually succeeded in adding to
the calm majesty of the stretch. In Ludlam's younger days
there had been no railway burrowing behind the crags. It
was not surprising that he had sat with his finger on the map.
Even out here in the sunshine, one had to know where the
gap was, if one did not want to miss a passing train. Brunt

walked for a quarter of a mile in a silence that was not a
silence at all. It was the sort of silence that a man could listen
to. There was a tranquillity, carried on a hum of insects, with
an occasional trout or chub rising to a fly. Then, where the
river curved, and the Georgian facade of the bottom mill
came in sight, Brunt saw George Ludlam sitting on the low
wall at the river's edge.

Even at a distance, the man's dignity and something of his
power seemed to make themselves felt. It was not only his
straight spine: there was something suggestive in the steadi-
ness with which he was taking in the view in front of him.
There was a conscious discipline, even in the relaxation of his
limbs.

He must clearly have seen Brunt approach, but showed no
sign of being disturbed. He made no move other than to turn
his face, which he did with an expression of interested
welcome.

'Good morning, Policeman. Do I flatter myself that reports and rumours bring you on my trail?'

'You might say that.'

Brunt sat down beside him.

'So who have you come here to protect? Them or me?'

'Do any of you need protection? I'm here to preserve the
Queen's peace.'

'Well answered. And if that is the case, you may confi-
dently withdraw. Neither they nor I are likely to upset our
sovereign's repose. I ask you, Mr What-ever's-your-name—'

'Brunt.'

'Mr Brunt—a name well borne. I ask you—and I fancy
you know something of my supposed adversaries—do you
think it likely that we shall come to blows? That they would
dare—or that I would bother?'

'Not by design,' Brunt said.

'I take that point.'

A dragonfly, a blue and green flash, momentarily motionless, caught a sunbeam, then darted away.

'On Sunday night, Mr Brunt, looking out through night, smoke and rain, you called this place beautiful; I took you to task for it.'

'And apologized. It must depend on what's in a man's mind when he looks at it.'

'It is beautiful. And yet, within sight of where we are sitting, I have seen a child hauled through the lodge on a rope's end to wash off the blood of a beating. That he did not die was due only to the human capacity for not dying. And the thing was not done as an example to others. It was done for the joy of doing it. One of the men who was involved in that incident has stopped coming to the Cordwainers' Arms because I am staying there.'

Brunt asked no names. The man said he was not here for vengeance, and showed no signs that he was planning any. A wagtail skimmed the water-edge vegetation.

'But I don't think they trust your intentions,' Brunt said.

'Then let them fear me. I hope it will do them good. If they go to bed terrified for a night or two, it's no more than I did for several tender years. But I repeat: I care nothing for them. It was places, not faces, that I came back to see. I hardly thought that the faces would still be here. As they are, I cannot help seeing them. But I assure you—my curiosity is detached.'

'I'm relieved to hear it.'

'So you may safely tell your superiors to call you off.'

There was something in Ludlam's tone that made Brunt wonder. Was he just a trifle too anxious to have him called off? He had said nothing about Eva Hargreaves. Brunt decided not to mention her for a while, to give Ludlam full opportunity to be frank of his own accord.

Presently they set off together back to Litton. Brunt suggested that he ought to respect Ludlam's desire for solitude, but Ludlam pleaded against it.

'No—please stay with me. I might at any moment see some reminder that is more than I can stand.'

Brunt referred to their conversation on Miller's Dale station, and asked how Ludlam had come to know that he was a policeman.

'From the way you were studying me. You were either the law or a confidence trickster weighing up a victim. And no trickster would allow himself to go about looking as unhappy as you were when you got into the carriage. I would say you betray too much in your eyes to succeed in your vocation. But maybe there is strength in an illusion of innocence.'

Once Ludlam's speech was tapped, he took pleasure enough in it. There was something stimulating in his mildly archaic turn of phrase. He stood and took a breath of the water-borne air.

'Yes—beautiful—today. Can you imagine what it was to be frightened by it? As a child of eight? Look at those crags. Think what creatures might be hiding behind them. Think of them under a black sky. What spirits haunt them? What is to stop them from toppling over on us without warning?'

As if playing into the hands of the pathetic fallacy, the dale chose at that moment to rumble in its depths, as if some immense subterranean predator were about to emerge. A slow, heavy goods train crossed the gap between the tunnels. Grey wisps of smoke clung to the water and a whiff of locomotive oil carried over to the two men.

'We came from St Pancras Workhouse,' George Ludlam said. 'Waifs, strays, abandoned. I never knew for certain which category I was. There were theories—they got lost when I was moved away from the people who might have known. But I can tell you that there came a time when the Pancras House of Industry seemed like some paradise of the past. We longed to go back there. There's your key to what Needham's mill was like. Even Nottingham—'

Ludlam paused, as if to ask himself whether he were talking too much. A few strands of smoke still lingered over the water.

'Nottingham?' Brunt prompted.

'We did not come straight from London to here. The original agreement was between the Pancras Poor Law overseers and a mill at Lowdham, near Nottingham. And by God, Nottingham was bad. I could vomit my heart up now when I think of the reasty smell of the oil on my hands as we ate boiled potatoes off bare wooden tables. No forks, no spoons, you understand, and meat only on Sundays. At least, they had enough imagination to call it meat. Bacon, Irish bacon, herring-fed, with the stink of our fingers to mix with the grease from the cotton-combings.'

A cabbage white butterfly, the first Brunt had seen this season, made a tentative movement, still drying her wings on a water-dock leaf.

'They didn't give us soap. Only a cake of meal once a week, with which we were supposed to scrub ourselves clean. It stands to sense that most of us ate it.'

There was a scent of water-level freshness, of wild mint, of nature unfolding in myriads of buds on either bank. They had come within sight of the corner-stones of the Litton mill. Ludlam stopped and spat into the water.

'I ought not to let it rankle. I got out of it and beyond it. But it was bad. At least in Nottingham we were bound by indentures. We had the promise that we would be taught frame-knitting, launched into the world with adult skills. Then they pushed us on to Needham's and the rules of apprenticeship went by the board. What Needham needed was labour dirt-cheap. They fed us enough to keep us alive. If you passed out through weakness at work you might, if you were lucky, be given a mug of warm water with treacle in it. That was to get you back to your bobbins. Were you ever thrashed, Mr Brunt?'

Brunt gave it a thought: punished as a boy; ill-matched in a rash fight as a youth.

'I was. Till the tatters of my shirt were as stained with blood as they were with black grease. I survived. At night I sometimes prayed to God that they wouldn't thrash me tomorrow. When they did, I stood up to it. Did you ever take pleasure in a thrashing, Mr Brunt? A sort of ferocious joy, because you are proving that they can't crush you? The only self-respect you had left was that they hadn't defeated you. And it wasn't only, or even mainly, the bosses who swung their belt-buckles. It was the men in between, the over-lookers, who were as scared of Needham and his sons as we were. A man called Billy Orgill was the last man to thrash me. I was thirteen. He was twenty-one or -two. Do you know Billy Orgill? When I caught sight of him, in Litton village on Monday morning, I burst out laughing.'

He laughed again now, but there was something hideous in the sound.

'So has the word got round to your Chief Constable's office that I've come back to get even? Can you see me knocking old men about on the street-corners of that Godforsaken hole?'

He stopped, and looked down at the mill-wheel.

'I used to know how fast that turned in a minute. Thirteen times, was it? A likely number. Thirteen revolutions a minute to keep a mainshaft turning. And from that shaft ran all the belts to the spindles and the roving frames. They set a pace that sixty kids must not lag behind. It was danger to the point of death if you didn't—as some proved.'

He was beginning to thunder like an agitator. Then he seemed to become aware of the excess of his passion; he subsided.

'Let's put these buildings out of our sight. They oppress me.'

So they came out of the mill gates into the unenclosed valley, where the river ran narrower and faster.

'And were there girls as well as boys in your Apprentices' House?' Brunt asked.

Ludlam seemed to see nothing personally pointed in the question.

'Girls? Aye—I can picture them now—A pale, hungry file in their oil-saturated bishops. Do you know what a *bishop* is,

Mr Brunt? It's a sort of shift: a sack upside down, with holes
for head and arms. I remember seeing them grabbing for
potatoes, those who'd been there a long time, the night I
arrived. There's something you expect from girls, isn't there,
Mr Brunt? A smile here, a tear there. These girls had neither.
They'd outgrown all that. They were greedy for potatoes.'
    'What happened to all these kids?'
    'What happened to them? Some ran away, and were
brought back to be flogged—as I was, more than once. Some
got away for good—like me, in the end. Some died. I never
heard that an inquest was held. They split the burials
between two parishes—Taddington and Tideswell. There
didn't seem quite so many, that way. Some were crippled,
and didn't survive. Some survived crippled—not always in
ways that met the eye. Maybe some even survived in their
bodily health and sanity. Who's to tell?'
    Still no mention of Eva Hargreaves, though their talk had
skated near her. So Brunt must introduce her himself. He did
not want the double walk to Litton village and back again.
    'So how many have you encountered, Mr Ludlam, of those
you used to know?'
    'Still clinging to your official brief, Mr Brunt?'
    'I am thinking of Eva Hargreaves.'
    'There was no one of that name at Litton in my time.'
    George Ludlam stood and looked at Brunt for some
seconds. Then suddenly his temper snapped, as it had done
on the train. He gripped Brunt's arms between elbow and
shoulder: an iron hold, painful and immobilizing. Brunt did
not struggle. He was conscious that he was failing in everything he had been taught about prestige and initiative.
Something told him that everything depended on maintain-
ing a personal relationship with this man, that this had only
temporarily gone astray. Ludlam's fingers gripped him
viciously.
    'What sort of country has England become? What sort of
police force is it that spends a man-morning on a personal

matter as far removed from a crime as an afternoon cup of
tea? On a friendship fifty years old, that never grew out of
childhood? Is this the case of your lifetime, Mr Unhappy
Policeman?'

Ludlam released him suddenly, his anger deflated. He
patted Brunt's arm.

'I lose my temper too quickly. It has had me in trouble
before. But ask yourself, Mr Unhappy Brunt: is this good
enough? Will this do? Do you harass a man because he takes
an interest in a crippled old woman?'

'It isn't just that,' Brunt said.

'What is it, then?'

Brunt was reluctant to give away strategical advantage.

'I expect you've heard the same sort of story in Litton
village as I have.'

'And do you believe these stories?'

'I don't know. I have to find out.'

'You can leave that to me,' Ludlam said. 'Believe me, if I
find there is a word of truth behind some things I have heard,
I shall have you back here by signal rocket if necessary.'

Ludlam twisted on his heel and was away up the steep hill
as if it had been level ground. Brunt followed the young river
up to Miller's Dale station. A haze of wild forget-me-nots
shimmered over the bank sides. He was hardly aware of
them.

CHAPTER 6

Brunt found Nadin so full of his own day's excitements that it
was difficult to bring his mind to bear on Litton.

Nadin had seen Amelia Pilkington, escorted by Sir William, go into a large jeweller's shop at the Terrace Road end
of Spring Gardens. She had taken a long time over her
choice. He had loitered outside and had heard the couple

arranging to meet for an afternoon tour by landaulette of the Dane Valley and Macclesfield Forest. But Amelia Pilkington was not on that landaulette. She was on the train that caught a London connection. Nadin hoped that Sir William had not been too extravagant: he had the look of a man who would nicely calculate the fair price for such favours as he had enjoyed. He would not go so far as to alter his will.

Jimmy Nadin revealed himself to his quarry for the first time that day as she was standing at the ticket-window, paying the single fare to Matlock. He touched her elbow lightly. Amelia Pilkington was a lady in her prime thirties who knew how to look demure, arch, piquante, outraged or audacious according to the exigencies of her current target. Today she knew that she was the target. She was tired—and candidly sour at the sight of Nadin.

'Not far enough, Miss Pilkington,' Nadin said.

'I beg your pardon?'

'Matlock's not far enough. Go somewhere outside the county boundary, please. Try Harrogate or Cheltenham. If I thought you were going to stay in our dales, I would have to write letters to colleagues all over the shire. That would mean extra work for them and another bout of frustration for you.'

She searched dramatically in her purse, as if counting her money.

'Would Le Touquet satisfy you?'

'Splendidly. You will not have to push your elderly friends up such steep hills.'

Nadin laughed. Brunt, still waiting his turn to speak, did not find the performance infectious.

'Well—tell me the troubles of Litton. You got it all out of Judson—eventually?'

Brunt had been mentally editing his report ever since parting from Ludlam. There were some things that he did not mean to tell, and other vital facts which he knew to his shame he had failed to unearth. He was still smarting from

the way Ludlam had humiliated him, and he did not care for
Nadin to learn about that.

'Oh—a man has come back who was one of the original
Poor Law slaves at the mill. A man who's done rather well for
himself, I'd say, though he had a bad time in the old days. An
interesting character—'

But what did Brunt know about him? His domicile, his
age, his walk of life—he had elicited none of these elementary
things. He had been held so spellbound that it was Ludlam
who had called all the tunes. But Nadin was not critical. He
was laughing again.

'Well—that's going to cause a bit of fluttering up there—
among those who have any plumage left.'

'Yes—a man called Billy Orgill, for one. He could have a
debt to pay—except that this stranger seems to be above all
that. And it appears there's a woman in the case—'

'Who's that, then, in Litton village?'

'Eva Hargreaves.'

Nadin had to think for a minute.

'I know. Ned Hargeaves's widow. Very clever man with
his hands, was Ned. Used to carve little ornaments out of
spar—little pigs and Derby rams. Used to sell them to
visitors. He left her not exactly well off, but better than many,
up Litton.'

'She's in none too good a way, and a couple called
Bagguley are looking after her.'

'*What!*'

Nadin had stiffened in his chair.

'Say that again, Tom Brunt!'

'A couple called Bagguley have apparently moved Eva
Hargreaves up to their farm—a place called Starve-Acre.'

Nadin was out of his chair now, involuntarily, moving like
a menagerie leopard that has caught the scent of the meat-
barrow.

'If only you knew, young innocent Tom Brunt, what words
are dropping from you. You'll have talked to Annie Barker?'

'I did—but is there any truth in what's said about these Bagguleys? I mean, a woman called Nell Merridew, who died aged ninety-seven, and people said she'd have lived to be a hundred?'

'She would have,' Nadin said.

'A man called Slack, who was supposed to have drunk spirits of salt?'

'He did drink spirits of salt.'

'Because he mistook it for gin,' Brunt said.

'Because he was meant to mistake it for gin.'

'Written off as accidental—'

'Because Pickford let it be. Because it was my case, not Pickford's. Because Pickford thought people would say he was listening to country gossip. Because Pickford saw himself being made an ass of in court. Because Pickford *is* an ass. Because Pickford's system is to make arbitrary decisions, then stand by them through thick and thin. Tom—we must get up there.'

'We've no other claim on tomorrow.'

'We've no stronger claim on tonight, lad. I see your friend Ludlam as a dangerous man.'

'Dangerous?'

'In Litton village any man with a brain is a danger—to himself, if not to the community.'

Brunt and Nadin arrived in Litton as late as any man can arrive there without having to walk the whole distance. Brunt had covered fourteen miles on foot today.

Their arrival was an occasion of some confusion. It seemed that since they had set out, some event of enormity had happened. Somehow, it was assumed that that was why they were here. And Judson did not begin the tale at the beginning.

'God knows, I'm no lover of the Bagguleys. But when they lay a complaint, it's got to run according to the book.'

'Steady, Jack—what's the complaint?'

'Only a break-in—at Starve-Acre. This stranger, this man

with the sea-chest, this Ludlam—'

'And what does he have to say about it?'

'Oh, he's gone. Down the hill with his chest on his back, in time to catch the six o'clock. But what was to stop him from hiding his box in Tideswell Dale, then working his way back under cover? And Eva Hargreaves is supposed to be his old lady-love.'

'And is she?'

'It's on everybody's lips.'

'It must be true, then,' Nadin said, his irony unappreciated.

'I know what I think, when sick people are taken care of by the Bagguleys.'

'And I know what I think, too. But there's got to be a sight more than thinking before anything goes down on paper.'

'Oh, paper—all some people think about is paper.'

'Paper has been known to save people from injustice.'

Jimmy Nadin talked so much in a spirit of mock cynicism, mock laziness and mock scorn that his earnestness now came as something of a shock.

'We'd better get straight up there, so I can show you the evidence. And God forgive me for putting us all to such trouble for the sake of the rights of the Bagguleys. But something tells me we've got to be careful.'

By moonlight they went up a stone-scattered farm track north of the village. The approaches and yard of Starve-Acre had about them a profligacy of muck: horse-muck, cow-muck, pig-muck, poultry-muck. There was debris of all kinds. Ben Bagguley had spasms of dealing in a variety of junk, and always seemed loath to part with any item of stock on the grounds of its unsaleability. Old copper boilers, old shed-doors, a mangle seized solid with rust: things stood about where they had arrived. Bagguley was a man of short-lived enthusiasms. He had a bank of coops intended for fighting cocks: but they were empty. So was a dovecot with sprung weatherboarding.

Judson demonstrated a triumph of detection as if it crowned his career. He showed with his bull's-eye where the paintwork of a window-frame, several decades old, had been violated by the blade of a knife. He showed how a window-catch had been forced against its stops, almost disembedding it from the woodwork. And by now the Bagguley pair, aggrieved, indignant, were crowding round, asserting their ownership of this evidence.

They all went indoors—an interior that was a consistent extension of the yard, the flagged floors protected by a covering of old sacking. The sole light was from the ragged wick of an oil lamp that had lost its glass chimney. The Bagguleys were wearing clothes that had arrived on their backs as other rejected property had arrived in their yard. There was a smell in the room—no more offensive than a country-bred person might find the floor of a rabbit-hutch—but strong, biting at the back of the throat.

The story was told with repetitions, emphatic phrases, protestations of outrage. Ben Bagguley had been out at the Red Lion at the time. He was not drunk—but he was rarely entirely sober. His wife was a red-cheeked, raw-wristed, bony-fingered woman, delighted to have recourse to the law now that it was unquestionably on her side.

She had gone over to a neighbour's to borrow what she called a twist of tea. When she had returned to Starve-Acre, it had been to find the back window broken open and a man in her kitchen, trying to find his way about with a lighted match. She had recognized him. He was that troublemaker who was staying at the Cordwainers'.

She looked to see whether this piece of provocation had any effect. It hadn't. They waited for her to go on.

He had been round this afternoon, making a nuisance of himself. Again, they did not ask the question that she was angling for.

So she told how she had seized Ben's gun from its corner. It was an ancient Bird's-gear muzzle-loader with a barrel four feet long. It hadn't been fired for a century, couldn't be, because half the firing mechanism was missing. Ben used it sometimes as a crowbar, up and down the farm, but usually it stood indoors for scaring off intruders.

It had certainly scared off this one. You should have seen the way he scuttled for the door when she dug him in the ribs with it. She tried to give a demonstration, but there were too many people in the room, and the guttering lamp was at risk. Nadin took the weapon from her.

So she had gone straight down the hill for Jack Judson. Because she was as entitled to have the Bobbies on her side as any other citizen, no matter what clacking tongues had made trouble for her in the past.

It came to Brunt that what he was witnessing was humanity at its least adorned. It was not just that the Bagguleys worked for sheer subsistence: what stood out was the meagre margin between survival and what they must look on as luxury. Were they criminals? How many in this village would abide by the law if they could gain a shilling without getting into trouble? If all was true about the Bagguleys that the village said—and clearly both Nadin and Judson believed that it was—then they were ready to commit crimes for a double figure of sovereigns. Suppose they deprived some old crone of her last few years: what could they hope from her? One decent chair, perhaps, for which Bagguley might find a market for a few pence. Perhaps one china cup and saucer, relic of a coming-of-age gift. Isaac Slack, for whom Molly Bagguley was supposed to have raised her skirts: that was an image to look at in the light of this dwelling. Didn't that leave Ben Bagguley open to a charge of living on immoral earnings? What immoral earnings? The price of a nip of gin, perhaps. Hardly enough to pay for the spirits of salt that were said to have got into the gin bottle. This was the raw material of humanity and crime, crudely chipped from the bedrock. And here were three trained and experienced officers, taking it as seriously as if they had caught Amelia Pilkington trying to defraud Sir William Palfreyman out of ten thousand pounds. They were taking it more seriously, in fact, because Jimmy Nadin was not playing for the laugh out of Molly Bagguley that he had had out of Miss Pilkington.

Sergeant Nadin waited until Molly Bagguley, having said it all, was beginning to say it all again.

'You said just now that this man is a troublemaker. What grounds have you for thinking that?'

'Isn't everyone saying so? Isn't Jack Judson saying so?'

Judson would not allow his eye to be caught.

'And you say he'd been here in the afternoon, making a nuisance of himself. What was all that about?'

'He wanted to see Mrs Hargreaves. I told him she was having her afternoon sleep. He tried to push past me into the house.'

'Did you tell him to come back some other time?'

She looked at Nadin with hatred: a woman of threshold intelligence, whose natural response to trouble of any kind was deceit.

'He'd know to do that, wouldn't he?'

'Did you suggest a time?'

'Why should I?'

'I want to see your lodger, Mrs Bagguley.'

'What has that to do with a man breaking into my kitchen?'

'Nothing, really, I suppose. After what has happened, Mrs Hargreaves couldn't be in safer hands.'

'What do you mean by that, Sergeant Nadin?'

'That you've just got to keep her alive now, haven't you?'

'Sergeant Nadin, I've slaved my nails to the quick for that woman. As I've done for more than one other. Who else in this village was willing to wait on Nell Merridew when she could no longer do for herself? Is there another soul in Litton who would have put up with Isaac Slack?'

'Mind you don't remind us of too much, Molly.'

'Remind you? Oh, I know you were after me, Jimmy Nadin. Well, this time the boot's on my foot. I'm not letting that Ludlam get away with this. I want him summonsed, Mr Nadin.'

'And I said, I want to see your lodger.'

'If you wake her, I shall be the one who has to sit up with her half the night.'

'Your privilege, Molly.'

She took an inch and a half of candle from the window-sill and lit their way up uncarpeted stairs. A different bouquet of smells emerged: a history of stale urine and faded human breath. The bedroom into which she showed them was clean by comparison with downstairs. Molly Bagguley must have foreseen this inspection and prepared for it according to her standards. The floor was carpeted with a double layer of reasonably clean old newspapers. Brown curtains, splitting with age, had been fastened across the window with a safety-pin. There was another stump of candle on the commode beside the bed, and she lit this from the one she was carrying. An old plough-handle was hanging by a rope from the ceiling, so that the patient could pull herself up in bed. But of the sleeping patient all that was visible was a concave cheek, of the texture of dried fishskin, and a tangle of thin white hair, against a ticking pillow that had no case. Molly Bagguley raised a corner of limp, greying sheet.

'Linen,' she said.

Eva Hargreaves's own outdoor coat was thrown over her as an eiderdown. She scarcely raised a contour under it.

'As I said, you've just got to keep her alive, haven't you?'

'I shall keep her alive. I shall have her up and about again.'

And this woman lying here was reputed to be better off than many in Litton—because her husband had carved little stone pigs for tourists. How much had Hargreaves left her, to put her in this class apart? Five pounds in gold pieces? Five gold pieces that the Bagguleys had their eyes on.

Ben Bagguley had the last word, the traditions of man-hood recurring to him.

'We want no messing about, now. We want this man found. We want him brought up at Bakewell. We want no capers like we've had before. We want this *known*, Mr Nadin.'

'You want it known that this caper's straight? It's got to be, hasn't it? And it had better be.'

They let themselves out into the chilly moonlight. There seemed to be a perceptible freshness, even about the muck in the yard. From the outlying houses of the village came a whiff of clean woodsmoke. Judson cleared rattling bronchial tubes.

'So what am I to do, Jimmy?'

'Do nothing, Jack. Make a noise doing it, if you've a mind to. If you feel obliged to go looking for George Ludlam, make sure you look in the wrong place. And if you do find his sea-chest, see that nobody knows you have.'

'Happen somebody will find it or him before I do.'

'In that case, you might have to make a few discreditable mistakes, Jack. Just try and make them seem natural. Because I want Ludlam at large. I don't want him moithered. I've got a feeling he's going to move in where Pickford wouldn't let me go.'

'I mind the time,' Judson said, 'when there was a boggart scaring folk at night, over up the Wardlow crossroads. Fellows like Dicky Lomas—'

But Nadin had had practice with Jack Judson.

'Come on, young Brunt. Let's go and see if Annie can find us beds for the night.'

CHAPTER 7

Annie Barker was not surprised to see them. Nor did she spare them her tongue.

'And I suppose if I was broken into, you would at least send young Brunt up before the end of the week. But if my name happened to be Bagguley—'

'Hold your noise, Annie Barker. It's five years come Michaelmas since I last got a chance to stick my nose into Starve-Acre—'

'I would have gone in backwards and left my nose outside. And what was it like underfoot? What are you going to do with your boots when you get home? Burn them?'

'Be no need. By the time we've finished tramping your carpets, they'll be clean enough for ceremonials.'

Annie had set a table for two with a three-pound slab of cold belly pork, potatoes and a half-stone jar of pickles.

'So you got to see Eva Hargreaves?' she asked, after they had started eating. 'Are you frightened of putting butter on your bread, Tom Brunt?'

Rolling towards him like an aproned Humpty-Dumpty, she spread his slice for him so that the butter squeezed down between his knuckles.

'Aye—we caught sight of Mrs Hargreaves. Bits of her, under the covers.'

'Up to her eyes in opium, I shouldn't wonder.'

'Now what special reason have you for thinking that, Annie?'

'Only that Molly was buying Dr Macmichael's Crescent Mixture down at Elsie Palmer's. I don't know why the law allows them to sell it.'

'Same law that allows folks to have aches and pains in their bones, I suppose. Yes—I thought I picked up a whiff of

Macmichael's, up in that bedroom.'

'You could pick that out, in Starve-Acre? No wonder they made you a sergeant.'

'And one of the reasons I've kept those three stripes is because I know little things like where George Ludlam is. Bring him out, Annie. I don't know where you've put him, but he's under this roof somewhere.'

'Nay, Jimmy Nadin, I'll take a dying oath—'

'Save your blasphemy, Annie, before you're struck off the planet.'

Nadin got up in leisurely fashion and began to go the round of Annie Barker's possessions, picking some of them up and examining them with a mixture of method and whimsy: a porcelain matchbox-holder in the form of a coach-man with a whip; a paper-knife with a handle in the shape of a goat's foot; a folding brass balance for test-weighing sovereigns. Then he moved her coal-scuttle an inch with the side of his foot, picked up the poker from one side of the fire and laid it down on the other.

Annie Barker finally chuckled.

'You're too clever by half, Jimmy Nadin.'

'You'd better square things up with your Maker, Annie, before you're struck with an everlasting palsy.'

'Nay, Jimmy. I swore he isn't under this roof. And he isn't, for sure. He's under the floorboards. Second cellar. It goes out from under the house.'

'Go and get him.'

'I don't know whether he'll come.'

'What was all that about?' Brunt asked.

'Copology,' Nadin said, his word for deliberate deception. 'People like to believe that we're clever. So I pick things up, look at them—and look as if they've told me something. Folks with something on their minds think I've got on to it. It was easy in Annie's case, because I know the little things she's proud of. I know what she'll have shown Ludlam. So I was handling the things he'll have handled. There's no vice in Annie. She couldn't hold out long.'

Annie brought Ludlam to them up a primitive staircase through a trap in one of her beer-cellars. A cobweb had attached itself to the bottom of his trousers and he retrieved a stalk of straw from his shoulder and flicked it on the fire. For all that, he still managed to appear distinguished—and looked as if he was ready to defend himself strenuously against verbal onslaught. Nadin got up and gripped his hand as if this were an overdue reunion with an old friend. He asked Annie to mix them all a hot toddy.

'I believe you've already met my friend Thomas Brunt.'

'Ah yes—our unhappy constable. We have discovered a number of things about each other.'

Ludlam seemed to react favourably at once to Nadin's impression of warmth and frankness. More copology? If so, Brunt was also among those taken in.

'Why do you keep saying I'm unhappy?' he asked.

'Well—don't you think he is, Sergeant?'

Ludlam looked at Nadin with a mischievous twinkle. Nadin examined Brunt comically, from an angle.

'No. It's news to me. I don't know what he's got to be unhappy about.'

Ludlam turned back to Brunt.

'Remember in the train? When I inferred you must be an investigator of some sort? It struck me how miserable you looked.'

The Sunday office interview with Pickford—

'So I said to myself, either that young man has suffered a disappointment with a lady-friend—or else he is not too happy in his job. And I don't know quite how to say this—I've no wish to be embarrassing—but one would not have said from the suit you were wearing that you'd been setting out lately to impress the ladies. Ergo, all is not as it might be in the young man's daily occupation.'

'Isn't it, Tommy?' Nadin asked him, taking advantage of Ludlam's ice-breaking skills. Brunt would be glad when they got on to some other subject.

'Not really,' he said. 'I sometimes feel as if I'm being pulled both ways at once. Like serving two masters.'

'We have it on unimpeachable authority,' Ludlam said, 'that no man can do that. The only master I serve is myself.'

'You didn't serve yourself any too well by breaking into Starve-Acre, did you?' Nadin asked.

'I suppose you're here to arrest me for that?'

'Not if I can possibly help it. Not if I can't find you. Not if you, with Annie's help, can keep out of my way. You'll understand, Mr Ludlam, that we are not sitting round this excellent fire, sipping these comforting drinks. Should the question ever arise in inconvenient places, there are three people here ready to swear bloodcurdling oaths that the present conversation has never taken place.'

Nadin looked first at Ludlam, then at Annie, confirming their understanding. He did not bother to look at Brunt.

'You'll go a long way in the police,' Ludlam said.

'That I shall not. I can now count in days the rest of my time in this force. And if certain people had foreseen the way I was going to develop, I would not have gone as far in it as I have. But with a little cooperation on your part, I shall go into civilian life feeling that at least one act of a drama has gone out on a rhyming couplet. Breaking and entering, by the way, is not the sort of cooperation I had in mind. Too many people take a sentimental view about the sanctity of a man's home—even if it be Starve-Acre.'

'I'm sorry. I was furious. They would not let me in to see her.'

'So, having got in, perhaps it's a pity you did not stand your ground.'

'She had a gun in my chest—the sort of weapon that can go off if you jerk it,'

'The sort of weapon that can't even be loaded. Ben Bagguley uses it for levering out tree-roots.'

'I was not to know that. I have done many things in my

life, but I have never paid attention to firearms. I've never needed to.'

'As a result of which, you did not get in to see Mrs Hargreaves. We did. And maybe I'm glad that you didn't, because I don't know what might have happened to your temper if you had. But you can be certain of one thing. The Bagguleys know that the pressure is on them. They are going to have to try very hard—'

'How can they try hard? That couple can't have the vaguest idea how to treat an invalid. Eva has to be got away from them. I've been trying to appeal to Mrs Barker here—'

Annie looked at them sadly.

'I can't, Mr Ludlam. Haven't I told you I can't? God knows, I'd do anything I could for Eva Hargreaves—or anyone else in bad straits. It would be hard, with an inn to run, but I'd try. But how can I pick and choose? If I did it for one, I'd have to do it for another. Is Eva the only woman in Litton who shouldn't be fending alone? What about Alice Fearn at Perry Top who's lost a leg with the sugar? What about my own cousin Ginny at Mason's Butts? I'd have to turn this place into a hospital. And where's the money for that?'

'I'm not without money,' George Ludlam said. 'Ten years from now, I can expect to be in my grave. I've no one to leave coin of the realm to.'

He looked again in appeal at Annie.

'I'm sure Annie's right,' Nadin said. 'Leave Mrs Hargreaves where she is for a day or two, while we look round to see what arrangements we can make. They've got her on opiates—these things can be bought over the counter by any Tom, Dick or Harry. She'll have to be weaned off them. We'll have to get a doctor in to her. She'll have to have a new bed and clean bedding—'

'Can't we get her back in her own home, and have her properly looked after there? I can pay.'

'Own home?' Annie asked. 'That's already let afresh.'

'What about her furniture, then—her odds and ends?'

'Advance payment to the Bagguleys—for services about to be rendered.'

'What—everything she has?'

'Don't overdo it,' Annie said. 'When Maggie Scrutton died, we were standing by watching. There'd been talk that King Midas himself couldn't have competed with what Will Scrutton had picked up at sales up and down. They sold it under the hammer on the pavement in front of her house. Twenty-five shillings the lot—including three chairs that went back before Queen Anne.'

Nadin made ugly sounds.

'And what had Isaac Slack got? A broken-handled chamberpot—and ten pounds in his mattress? That's what the Bagguleys killed him for. And I let Pickford call me off. He said he'd have me out of the force if I made a fool of him over what he called peasant gossip.'

'You should have taken a chance, Jimmy,' Annie said.

'Well—I'm taking one now.'

Ludlam stirred in his chair.

'I'm not playing games with Eva, Sergeant Nadin, just so that you can settle an old score.'

'It isn't only on my account that I'm settling it.'

Nadin picked up the poker and edged back a coal that had fallen against the bars.

'Mr Ludlam—I don't know where Eva Hargreaves is placed in your life. If you don't care to tell us, we shan't press you—'

CHAPTER 8

'It's a funny thing,' George Ludlam said. 'You might say Eva was never anything to me at all. Or you might say we were only children—so how could there have been anything be-

tween us? But I've never been one to take that view. Male
and female, boy-girl, man-woman—everything between
them is affected by the fact that one's a man and one's a
woman—even if it's only two pairs of eyes catching sight of
each other on a railway station.'

Annie had made up a fire that would see them through
another hour.

'I was a strange little boy—I must have been—when I first
became aware of myself in Pancras Workhouse. I'm not
saying that I was better than anyone else. I was different. I
couldn't help being different. How was I different? For one
thing, I had a different way of seeing things. If I looked at a
kettle, or a ladle, or a gentleman's walking-stick, then I used
to think those things had characters of their own. It wasn't
quite like investing them with a human personality. It was as
if I thought that all things had a soul—but not a man's soul: a
kettle's soul, or a walking-stick's soul.'

He looked at Annie Barker's mantel clock, which had a
glass panel with a view of an Alpine village.

'That clock has a soul. It's one of a thousand clocks, all
made from the same materials, and to exactly the same
pattern. But that clock has lived all its life in this room. It
has, as it were, seen everything that's happened here. So it
isn't quite the same as a precisely similar clock that has lived
somewhere else.'

'I see what you mean,' Annie Barker said.

'No. I don't think you do. I don't see how you can.'

This was strange: authoritative, uncompromising. Annie
was visibly taken aback.

'I am telling you this, not because I claim it is a philosophy, but because I want you to see what sort of a mind I
had as a child. I was always lonely in the crowd. I would look
at things—at all things—and wonder. Other people looked
at things and did not even see them.'

He felt in his pocket for pipe and tobacco, produced a
mellowed calabash that seemed to add to his air of apartness.

'The trouble was, I did not really know in those days how different from each other people were. I talked to everyone as if their minds worked in the same way that mine did. I don't mean adults. You only got to speak to adults in Pancras Workhouse if you were in trouble. I mean I talked to other children—some of them distinctly not philosophers, and not given to human charity for its own sake. Not in Pancras Workhouse.'

Ludlam had forgotten to draw on his pipe. He put a fresh spill to it.

'I used to think that one day I'd write a book to tell the world the rottenness of Pancras Workhouse. Yet only this morning I was telling young Mr Brunt how we longed to be back there, after they'd shipped us to these northern mills. Of course, you don't keep a random community in order without discipline. But I've found out—and it's as true in Litton village today as it was in Litton Mill half a century ago—that it isn't from the people set over you that your worst troubles come. It's from those you have to live with.'

He clearly did not expect comment, and no one interrupted him.

'To a large extent, of course, my troubles were my own fault. I talked to people, as I say, as if their minds worked as mine did. I said daft things about door-handles and bedrails. They thought I was mad, and they tormented me. I liked believing the things that people told me, so I was a very easy young person to tease. I believed them when they told me that we had a traditional ration of shrimps for tea on Good Friday, and I got my ears boxed for going to the store to ask for my dormitory's share.'

He laughed, but it was without humour.

'I was different—even if that only meant that I was daft—but I liked to believe that I had a secret superiority. I liked to connect this in a melodramatic way with my parentage—about which I knew nothing. But there was gossip among some of the domestic workers—they always stopped talking about me when they saw that I was stretching my ears. There was something special about my father, and one day something special was going to happen to me.'

Annie Barker was following this avidly. Her eyes were watching every nuance of his face, and her overfed lips were moving silently, as if she were telling the story herself.

'Well, something did happen. They packed fifty or sixty of us into wagons and sent us trundling up to Nottingham.'

Jimmy Nadin was resting one temple against the ball of his thumb, and his eyes were closed as if in sleep. But Brunt had seen that posture of concentration before, and knew that the sergeant was not missing the innuendo of a syllable.

'I don't blame the St Pancras Poor Law overseers over-much—and yet I can't pronounce them free from guilt. They did not know what they were doing to us—yet they could have got to know. They were deceived. They thought that they were sending us bound to learn a useful trade. They went to bed happy. All I can say is, they were a little too ready to go to bed happy.'

He tamped down the ash over his core of tobacco.

'It was exhilarating at first, rattling out through Radlett and St Alban's: red cows in green fields. Some of us had not exactly had a surfeit of green fields. Of course, our wagon was covered, so that the public could not see us passing. But there was a crack in the woodwork where I was crouched. We sang, I remember, a ditty that had grown up out of nobody's and everybody's throat, to the tune of one of the old street cries:

> Oh here come the Pancras spinners,
> Copping the lot, copping the lot.

It was a bit different when two or three started to be sick from the jolting on the rough roads. And we didn't finish that journey in the course of a day. A night in a barn—and nobody had thought of providing blankets.'

Brunt reached for what was left of his toddy.

'Nottingham. Lowdham Mill. And I told you, Mr Brunt, Lowdham was paradise, compared with Litton. The first thing that struck my eye were those lines of girls in their bishops, scrabbling for potatoes on the rough wooden tables. And sitting among them—half a head taller than most of them—she was ten and I was eight—Eva Lorimer—narrow features, sharp, crafty eyes, hair straggling, arms fleshless, fingers dirty and busy. They hardly talked at first. The only way to make sure of your food was to get it into you. But when their mouths were full, and there was nothing left to scrabble for, some of them started talking—except for one or two who'd gone to sleep with their faces on the table. I remember one girl had her cheek in the salt-pile. And I heard Eva Lorimer's voice, shrill, ringing out above the rest. A London voice—these girls had come up a couple of months before us.'

'She's never lost that voice,' Annie Barker said.

'Well, the first night was purgatory, trying to sleep in all our clothes under one blanket in double bunks. The first day's work was unqualified hell. We were at it, and getting licked by belts' ends before they'd properly told us what we'd come here to do. Six in the morning till ten at night. My initiation into the cotton trade was to clear the waste from the floor—and that meant from under the machinery, because I was small enough to crawl there. And there were moving parts that could knock a boy silly if he did not look lively. And it meant a few more cuts across your back, if that put you behind with your work. I remember keeping half a crust back from my breakfast, so that I could pay a boy to let me lean on his shoulder on the way back to bed.'

It was a long cry to the tall man in the well-cut suit in Annie Barker's best chair.

'That's what life was like—but I had Eva Lorimer. It was love at first sight—and I am not making a joke about that. We were hardly out of infancy, and it had nothing to do with merit, or character, or beauty—praise Heaven, we were too filthy to be beautiful. This was the real thing, as I understand love between man and woman to be—all-consuming, and based on nothing. What did I want with her? To have her to myself and be her only friend. To rescue her—oh, not from giants and dragons, but from Lowdham, Litton, to fly with her down some of the more luscious valleys that we had seen on our way up here.'

Nadin opened one eye and looked at the story-teller—a shrewd, ungullible eye, that gave nothing away of its opinions. Then he shut it again, with a little nod to Ludlam to go on.

'The oddest thing is that I can't say in honesty that there was anything desirable about Eva. I don't think she would have been pretty, even if you could have cleaned her up. If she had had it in her to make a graceful movement, she wouldn't have thought it worth making. She wasn't kind. We were all too unhappy for kindness. Like everybody else, she worked till she couldn't work, to keep herself out of worse trouble. Just now and then she would kick over the traces, throw a tantrum, speak her mind, irrespective of the consequences. In that respect, she was one of the worst offenders in the mill.'

'She hasn't changed,' Annie Barker said.

'And—I never let it truly cast me down—she had no room for me at all. If I was an oddity in the eyes of the Pancras kids, I was the laugh of the universe for the older ones, from other London workhouses, who had got here before us. They looked on themselves as the experienced generation. Eva had a louder voice than most, and it was the one that most of them listened to. There was no namby-pamby tolerance about Eva. She had no room for anything that wasn't in her own image. And the greater her contempt for me, the more I wanted to impress her. Pathetic, isn't it? When I was knocked off a ladder by a swinging frame-end, she was the one that I wished hadn't seen it happen. When John Needham lifted me higher and higher off the ground by the hairs of my scalp, and asked me if I could see London yet, I heard Eva laughing.'

He laughed himself, an effort at self-deprecation.

'John Needham, yes—I am coming to Litton. They brought us to Litton because somebody's money had run out at Lowdham. You'll be tired of hearing me say this: Litton, thanks to Ellis Needham, made everything else pale that had ever happened. That dale, Mr Brunt, that you called beautiful—we were sucked up between those crags as if we were being shepherded into an etching for Dante's *Inferno*.'

For the third time, George Ludlam laughed—but this time it was wholly theatrical.

'That nearly made you open your eyes again, didn't it, Sergeant Nadin? To think that I know about Dante? Well, I didn't in my Litton days, that's for sure. I did know what it was to be fined a morning's pay for letting my bobbins get ahead of me. I did know what it meant to be thrashed by Billy Orgill—because Billy Orgill had to let the Needhams see that he was doing the job that they were paying him for. And I did learn to fight back, even if fighting back could not possibly do anything but make matters worse.'

He leaned forward and tapped Nadin on the knee. Nadin opened an eye, but did not change his posture.

'Then one day a couple of Overseers from the St Pancras Poor Law came up on a visit. I don't know what had got into their consciences. It might seem ironical to suggest that they had any. In fact they had—and they had their moments of activity. The trouble was, they knew too easily how to quieten them down again. They weren't bad men, Mr Nadin. They had good ideas—a few. But they were very easily satisfied that they had put them into effect. Coming up to Litton was one of their better notions. And it did us a little good. Ellis Needham and his sons must have had their consciences too. They made one or two sorry attempts at covering up—fresh oatcakes, with a smear of treacle on them, on a weekday! A few dozen new blankets spread out

over the tops of the worst-looking bunks—and collected in
again after the visitors had gone. But those Overseers must
have seen something that made them uneasy. If they didn't,
they were deaf, blind and dense. Of course, the kids they
talked to only wanted to please, and it had been drummed
into us in our Pancras days that contentment was the
Christian way of rewarding our benefactors. Every child
there knew that they had to go on living under the Needhams
after the Overseers had reported back satisfactorily to the
Board of Guardians.'

Ludlam was no mean orator. He knew how to lead up to a
vital point.

'You've read of Oliver Twist. I was the boy who asked to
be taken before the Overseers. I could see Needham's eye
warning me that I would pay dearly for any trouble that I
made for him. Every other kid was doing his best to show that
he wasn't associated with me. Eva was smirking. They all
believed I was signing my own execution warrant.

'But those two Pancras Overseers were prepared to give
me a hearing. One of them was a younger man—well, I'd put
him lower than forty—with a fancy, gilt-braided waistcoat. The other, who had remarkably little to say, was
an older man with a paunch and a way of patting it as he
listened.

'I asked them two things, and the first was what had
happened to our bonds of apprenticeship. They asked me
how old I was, and when I said ten, they told me I hardly
need think of starting my journeyman years yet. But I knew
what I was talking about. I had listened to older hands, who
had found themselves equipped for nothing when they ought
to have been out of their time. The young man in the
waistcoat told me that it would be looked into.

'Then I asked about being beaten. A boy had almost died
from being thrashed for trying to abscond. I was told that a
boy who tried to run away must expect a beating. But what, I
tried to ask, about beating a boy beyond the limits of humane

entitlement? I did not put it into those words, but I believe they understood what I meant. They asked me the name of the boy who had been so beaten, but he had prayed me not to give it, believing that he would be flogged even worse. I was told that I could not expect to be taken seriously if I were unable to furnish evidence. Mine would then be a frivolous complaint, for which I could expect only one kind of treatment. They assured me, however—brimming with humanity as they were after a session at Ellis Needham's midday table—that they would not report my disloyalty to my master—provided that I would either substantiate my accusations or withdrew them.

'This I refused to do, and I said that I was worried in case I should one day be beaten to death.

' "Why, boy—are you thinking of absconding?"

' "No, sir. In this mill a boy does not need to abscond to be beaten beyond endurance."

' "Have you been beaten beyond endurance?"

' "Several times, sir."

'The younger man looked at me, not unkindly. But however liberal-minded he wanted to be, he could not forget that he was a man of status.

' "All I can say is that you seem to be enduring pretty well. But I would not like to leave you with the impression that your masters can get away with anything they like. Should you ever—or any of your companions—suffer the sort of treatment you are trying to convince us of—you have the same remedy as any other citizen of this realm. You can call on the protection of a Justice of the Peace."

'I had no very clear idea in my head what a Justice of the Peace was, but I thanked him.

' "Anyone will show you the way to one. That is something that no one can deny you. But I should warn you that if you go to the magistrature with anything less than a cast-iron case, the repercussions will be memorable."

' "Yes, sir."

'"Bearing false testimony would be no light charge, Master Ludlam."

'They went away. And so did Ellis Needham's treacle-tins. So much for the philanthropy of this noble century. But I now had a second figure to rank alongside my idealized Eva: the English rural Justice.'

Ludlam took several deep breaths. Annie Barker got up and offered to recharge his glass. He declined, and so did Nadin. Brunt, feeling oddly independent, accepted. Annie did not pour him much.

'There was a punishment at Litton for infringements—half an hour for girls, an hour for boys. You had to stand under one of the frames with a bucket of water in each hand. They had wooden blocks for you to stand on, according to your height. And you had to bend pretty low to avoid being hit on the head when the frame swung back and forth. I was given more than one spell of it, as you can imagine, and I can tell you, it got pretty painful, bending forward from the waist, and four gallons of water got pretty heavy, when you had to straighten up with them in a hurry. Once or twice I got into the rhythm of it for most of my spell, but when you began to get tired, you were bound to have your skull cracked a time or two.

'Eva had earned a spell for some back-answer she had given, and when she followed it up with another, she was given the full hour. This made a lot of people catch their breath. Even by the Needhams' yardstick, an hour for a girl was excessive. We daren't, of course, stop work to watch, but a lot of eyes were not on what they were supposed to be doing. That's one of the things I hate most about communal suffering: when some one else is in trouble, it does vary the monotony of the others.

'I can still see Eva Lorimer as she stood there defiant, taking the weight of the buckets with her elbows against her sides. She'd a flash in her eyes for anyone who looked her way—John Needham included. I knew how she felt. I've spoken before about enjoying a beating. Well, you don't, of course. You can only persuade yourself that you're achieving something—showing the rest of them that it means nothing to you. Eva had not had as much practice under the beams as some of us had. It took her some time to get into the motion. She was a tall girl, so they only had her on one block, but even at that, the woodwork caught her more than once across the shoulder-blades, knocking her on to her knees with the buckets flying. They had to be filled up again, and John Needham kept calling for extra time. When she'd finished, she staggered back to her working post—and no one dared leave his to help her. She was on piecing, one of the most detested tasks, because you had to mend broken threads, and they had a habit of happening all at once. And if your mind wandered, you could upset the whole process. Eva hardly knew how to get back to her spindles. Her limbs were shrieking for rest. She was dizzy. And that's how she fell into the driving-belt, got her leg between the webbing and the lower wheel. I don't know which came first—her scream or the crack of her thigh-bone. Someone—it was one of the overlookers, God bless him—got bad brush-burns, hauling the belt off the shaft. Eva was one of the few cases I know where a doctor was actually called in to a child-worker. And even at that, Needham didn't mean to lose what he'd spent on fees. They tell me Eva was back piecing within a few months.'

Ludlam was silent for some seconds, awaiting the effect of his story. That and something else: something else was happening to him—a surge of uncontrolled rage. He rose to his feet, thumped his left fist into his right hand and thundered.

'That's why, by God, I've no room for a society that will not stick together for its simplest rights. There was no one—no one but a boy of eleven—to speak up for Eva Lorimer. There was no mention, of course, in any official report, of how she came to stumble into that machinery. I did my stupid little best, and I failed. And I hadn't the guts to try to follow up failure with a second attempt. Instead of staying to fight—at the age of eleven—I made my getaway—thanks to outside forces that I did not deserve. That's why—'

His tone softened. He was a man whose rages did not last long.

'That's why, when I came back here—out of sentimental curiosity, no more—I had no thought of finding Eva Lorimer still here. Of course, I have no feelings for the woman now—not man-about-woman feelings. But I remember the feelings I used to have for her. And the feelings I would have for any soul who went through what Needham put us through—only to be battened on by the likes of the Bagguleys. I haven't come to the end yet. Shall I go on?'

CHAPTER 9

George Ludlam was a good story-teller, spacing his points, honestly qualifying them, quietly assuring himself that they had gone home, sandwiching them with the odd maxim from his philosophical ragbag. He kept coming back to his theme of a community that passively accepted its miseries.

'I couldn't, of course, find the words for it then that I can now—but I *felt* it, I tell you. I'm not saying that I was a noticeably clever youngster, but I had a sense of justice. I knew what Needham and his managers would do about Eva's accident. The first thing was, they had to keep her alive if money would buy that—because a death after that kind of accident could have meant a bristling inquiry—especially if the news of it drifted down to St Pancras. Needham and his lieutenants moved about with softer tongues than usual among those who had been in the spinning-room when the accident had happened. They had to make sure of the gap between what the children had seen, and what they would

say they had seen. Those kids were as singly-directional as a
flock of sheep—and just about as woollen. Nobody wanted to
have seen anything. They had all been concentrating on their
own work. I tried to recruit support, mostly from boys older
than myself. It was about what they expected of me. I was
mad, irresponsible—I would bring unimaginable new
horrors down on all of us. It was all in the words of that
lunatic ditty we had sung on the way here:

> Here come the Pancras spinners,
> Copping the lot, copping the lot.

We were copping the lot. It was our lot to cop the lot.'
   In vain did young George Ludlam try to tell people about
Justices of the Peace. Justices of the Peace might exist—but if
they did, it was for themselves, for a different sector of the
world, not for Pancras spinners. Justices of the Peace could
only wish more woes on Pancras spinners than they knew
already.
   George Ludlam decided to act alone. His first feat had to
be to break out of his quarters, itself a monstrous risk. The
Apprentices' House was a heavily barred barracks. It was
not patrolled at night. It did not need to be. Once the bars
were behind their iron brackets, the place was sealed.
Moreover, for some devious reasons of Needham's concerned with Poor Law boundaries, it was on the opposite, the
Taddington, side of the river. Anyone attempting to cross the
bridge was hopelessly vulnerable.
   Ludlam got out by the expedient of not going in. It meant
sidling away from the pack, as if for a call of nature, while
they were on their way from the mill at the end of the day. It
meant hiding in a loathsome place—a dank, slimy alcove in
the flank of the weir that fed the waterwheel. It meant
crouching there, cramped and shivering, while he heard the
hue and cry for him going on on the banks and in the woods
above him. Dusk was on his side. His body and clothes had

taken on the same shade of green as the walls against which
he was leaning. Some of his searchers must actually have
looked down into the weir without seeing him.

He waited until he heard the great bars of the barracks
being wedged into position, then schooled himself to be
patient for another half-hour. He emerged into a dark night,
a quarter-moon largely behind clouds, only the faintest of
luminescence reflected from irregular patches of water. The
dale with its sentinel crags can seldom have looked more
frightening.

He climbed out of the dale without any real notion of
where he was heading. He went up through Litton Slack and
the village, snoring and supine. Hungry—he had had to miss
his evening meal, for what that was worth—he came into the
open, scarred hill-country overlooking Peak Forest and Cave
Dale. Somewhere—he judged in some town, but he did not
know where to look for a town—there must be a Justice of the
Peace, who would listen and make scandalized clucking
noises at the story he was going to hear.

George Ludlam did not find a Justice of the Peace that
night, but he came a stage nearer to one the next morning,
when a couple in a cottage took pity on him and asked him in
for a breakfast of bread and dripping and hot tea. But this
temporary haven turned into a narrow escape. He overheard
something that told him that they were tricking him to stay
until they could get in touch with the Needhams. There
would be a reward for a returned apprentice.

Ludlam sneaked out of the back door, and with an instinct
for fieldcraft worthy of Fenimore Cooper, started to make his
way towards Chapel-en-le-Frith, having learned in the cottage that the town was a seat of justice. He had heard the
name of one of the principal magistrates of the district,
Parson Septimus Wheatley.

Jimmy Nadin moved a limb.

'Aye—and you'll find a Wheatley still on the bench. The
Reverend Bartleby Wheatley, Rector of Hucklow Gate and

Rural Dean. Old Septimus's son, and no friend to poor men. You'll do well to stay out of trouble anywhere within Bartleby's sphere of influence, Mr Ludlam.'

'I dare say. And I'd have done well to have avoided his father too. I found my way to the parsonage, and my first scrape was with an elderly woman who would not allow me into the house because of my filthy appearance. She made me go round to the back door and talk to her from outside. Then she went in and spoke to the Reverend, and when she came out again, he had evidently told her to get the gist of my story from me. I gabbled a fast and confused narrative, and she made indignant noises and said she was sure that the Reverend would want no truck with an apprentice who was going against his master.'

Parson Wheatley came to the door himself shortly after that, a massive, white-haired, barrel-chested, thundering man, still dressed in clothes of eighteenth-century cut, who struck Ludlam tongue-tied with awe. Try as he may, the boy could not say the things he wanted to say, could not suppress the things he knew would be better suppressed, could not produce a balanced version of events. All he could keep repeating was that a girl had been terribly injured and would probably die, and it had all happened because she had been treated in such a way that—

The parson blasted him with words.

'You are trying to lay an information, boy? But what is your information? I can make neither head nor tail of it. Before I can hear a complaint, it must be put into proper legal language. What law do you say has been violated? I know of none. Accidents will happen in factories and mills. And I must warn you, young sir, that if you cannot support your complaint, the day will go hard with you. A man's master is his master. Go and see my clerk. There will be a Justices' court in Chapel-en-le-Frith on Thursday. Perhaps Jenkins will arrange for you to be heard then.'

Jenkins was a solicitor. It was late in the day before

Ludlam reached him—and he was no more inclined to take Ludlam's side than the vicar had been.

'Without evidence? It seems to me you have no evidence. You must go back to Litton and recruit witnesses, or drop the whole notion of any action. You have put yourself totally in the wrong by coming away like this from your master. I take it you are indentured?'

'No proper notice is taken of the indentures.'

'You cannot know what you are talking about. You must go back to Mr Needham.'

'But if I go back to Mr Needham, he will have me thrashed till I cannot stand.'

'He would not dare lay a finger on you while you have an action before the bench. Later, when your action has failed— as I am bound to give you my opinion, it surely must fail—'

'Then can you not give me a paper, to give Mr Needham, that he is not to thrash me?'

'I can give you no paper. Come back with your witnesses, and if their evidence has substance, we will engross a summons, and when Parson Wheatley has signed it—'

Ludlam moved his chair a few inches nearer the fire, which was beginning to fall in on itself.

'I told you I was mad. I went back to Litton Mill. I had faith. I still believed that there was a system over and above us, and that if we stuck hard to our beliefs, right would be with us in the end. Ellis Needham was one of the first to see me when I walked back into the mill compound. He laughed with joy at the sight of me.

'"Well, here's one at least who knows which side his bread's buttered. Bring him over here, so that we can butter it a bit more for him."

'"Mr Needham, you have no right to thrash me. Mr Jenkins says so."

'"And who's Mr Jenkins?"

'"The Clerk of the Justices."

'And I said the Reverend Wheatley's name, and told him

that a summons was going to be made out, and that until the case had been heard—

'Ellis Needham was standing behind me. I could hear the anger in his breathing and the creak of the whip in his hand as he flexed it. I stood and waited for the first lash.

'But it did not fall. Maybe the power of the law was such that Needham grasped in the nick of time that he had to accept it. I think, though, that he held his hand for reasons of broad strategy, for next morning he did thrash me. I expect he had been in touch with Jenkins and Wheatley, had made sure of the way the case would go with him—if there ever were a case. The Justices were on the side of the masters and there was no hope—it was the foolishness of my age ever to have believe that there could have been hope—that Joe Moss, Peter Townley, Dick Logan and Harry Lockett would take an oath in a witness-box and say what they had seen done.

'They thrashed me, and work was stopped at the spindles so that St Pancras, Bethnal Green and all the other London workhouses could make a hollow square and see example made. I played my usual game of showing them that I could stand up to it, but the flesh could not take the punishment that was inflicted this time. When I came to, I was lying in my own bunk, deserted, and the daylight was riddling in through the ill-fitting shutters. It was only in final physical collapse that any child was ever allowed to lie there during working hours.

'I lay for perhaps three-quarters of an hour, perhaps longer, before making an effort to sit up. Half an hour later, I was free of the dale again. It was easier by daylight. There was no supervision of the barracks because as a rule there was no one there to supervise. I made my way a little upstream and got out of the mill grounds by a gully occupied by emaciated, self-sown hawthorns—and a family of chaffinches whose indignation I thought might give me away.

'I escaped a second time from Litton Mill, but my progress

was poor, and if I had not run into help, I would undoubtedly
have been recaptured that same day. I was a boy of eleven,
you must remember, and my tender youth, as it must, was
now calling the tune. Tender, in fact, is a neat word for my
condition. There were places where I could not bear my shirt
to touch my back, others where it was stuck to the weals as if
by horse-glue. I ran, as I say, into help. It was help that was
to draw the shape of the rest of my life for me. But that is
another story. It has nothing to do with anything that has
happened, or will happen, in this village. I'm sure we are all
ready for bed. So let us leave me where I had got to by sunset
that night: an inn on a highroad. Abandoning my lady-
love—that thought often came into my head—deserting my
friends. This still troubled me. I still believed that if only I
had tried hard enough, I could eventually have talked sense
into them and got them to make common cause. I have
caught sight of a few familiar faces in this village in the last
few days, and the only common cause they have made is an
abject surrender to circumstance.'

George Ludlam was not up and about when Nadin and
Brunt were ready to leave the next morning. Nadin told
Annie Barker not to disturb him and not under any per-
suasion to allow him to try to leave the house in daylight
hours.

The pair returned to Buxton. Brunt had to attend to the
case of a lady who had left a purse behind in the wicker chair
in which she had been wheeled to take the waters, and whose
attendant claimed no knowledge of it. Brunt interviewed the
man, who now remembered having put it on one side in the
hope of coming across his fare again. An outrageous lie—but
he was a poor man, and only occasionally a rogue, so Brunt
dissuaded the plaintiff from laying a charge.

Nadin had to go to Hartington to look into the alleged theft
of some expensive fishing-gear from a gentleman who had
come to cast a fly in Beresford Dale. It turned out to be a

complicated case, with other men's rods and creels also missing. Nadin was away from Buxton for three days, and during that period Brunt lacked any news of what might be happening in Litton.

Then he ran into Tommy Lamp-oil, who had come down to the railway goods yard to collect a consignment. Tommy told a tale of good-neighbourly activity in Litton. Annie Barker, too breathless and obese these days to venture far beyond the yard of the Cordwainers' Arms, had nevertheless struggled up to Starve-Acre with a heavy basket on her hip (Annie Barker's hip?) delivering clean bedlinen and nutritious food. There had been an epic verbal battle between her and Molly Bagguley, but that was a contest that no one would expect her to lose. Nothing more had been seen of George Ludlam. His sea-chest had not been found, and it was concluded that he must have succeeded in spiriting himself out of the region.

But Litton village was not famous for its goodwill for long. There was a sudden tumult of messages coming and going out of the Buxton police offices. Nadin and Brunt were sent for and ordered to make their way up to Litton as fast as horse and steam could carry them. A woman called Molly Bagguley had been most atrociously murdered. PC Judson had raced down to Miller's Dale station, where for the first time in his life he had sent a telegraph message to Derby. Inspector Pickford had arrived in Litton in record-breaking time—for murder is the pinnacle of crimes, even for Inspectors who have been Captains. The brief word that reached Buxton was that he had arrested a man called George Ludlam. There was an implicit suggestion that Ludlam had been caught more or less red-handed.

CHAPTER 10

Nadin had a word in Brunt's ear.

'We saw nothing of Ludlam, the night the Bagguleys were broken into. That goes without saying. Ludlam won't let us down. I don't know what's happened. He might have had one of his fits of temper. But if he's innocent, he'll know that only you and I can save him from Pickford.'

Brunt saw what he meant, but he wished that life were simpler. And something of that thought must have shown in his face.

'Of course,' Nadin said, 'if we do drop in the dirt, I take the battering. You're a youngster working under my orders.'

But Brunt knew that superior orders would not cover such blatant irregularities as this. They were unlawful orders, and that was the end of any excuses; the end, too, of any thought of a career in the Force.

'No. I'm with you on square terms, happen what might,' he said.

'That's daft talk. If it goes sour on us, you'll have to turn to quarrying stone. If we can save the day, you'll be in line for three stripes on your sleeves when I go.'

For some reason which only he knew, Pickford had brought Ludlam back to Litton from his remand cell, handcuffed to one of his Derby constables. Immediately he saw the Buxton pair, he had Ludlam transferred to Brunt's wrist while he went round the corner with Nadin. It was some time since the pair had been in each other's company, and there was much miscellaneous ground to be covered, going over some months of characteristic Nadin casework.

Brunt and Ludlam were unequal in height and neither of them had had much practice at being in irons. There were some painful moments before they learned to co-ordinate their movements. Fortunately, Ludlam seemed to have some ability as a ventriloquist. No casual observer could have known for certain that he was talking.

'I'm relying on you two. God knows, there's no one else on my side.'

'What happened?' Brunt asked.

'If I knew that, it's someone else who'd be facing what I'm facing.'

'The Inspector doesn't seem to be in any doubt.'

They could hear the rise and fall of Pickford's voice, not what he was saying. Nadin seemed to be taking no great part in the dialogue.

'Tell me the whole story.'

'Stop talking to him, Brunt!'

Pickford was back, Nadin behind him, making faces at Brunt to show how little he cared about whatever had been said.

'Bring him this way.'

Now they set out up the steep street at the northern end of the village. There was a silence about Litton, even an emptiness in the open spaces. The population had gone to earth. But there could not be many pairs of eyes in the place that were not looking on from somewhere, and when it was seen that they were heading for Starve-Acre, it was too much for the general curiosity. Clusters of grey-clad, round-shouldered figures appeared in the distance behind gates and from round the corners of rough-chipped lime-stone walls. Some of them advanced ten, twenty unconfident paces.

Judson, his uniform belt barely holding in a gut like a meal-sack, glowered back at the vanguard of the sightseers. He made no motion with his spade-like hands. It would have been superfluous. Litton knew what Judson meant, what later unpublicized reprisals would lay in store for contraventions. Judson was master of Litton village. A pity, Brunt thought, that Pickford had not witnessed that moment of silent command. But Pickford was the striding leader, a pace or two ahead that no one cared to bridge: that might have involved them in conversation with the Inspector.

The contrast between Pickford and Ludlam was striking. Ludlam, being an unconvicted prisoner, was still in his own clothes—the suit and caped coat in which Brunt had first seen him on the train. And despite the constrictions of cell life, he had still managed to keep himself in faultless trim—which made Brunt think again of the ingrained military man. But Ludlam was not opulent, and Pickford was. Pickford's shoulders were padded. His greatcoat was cut to make the most of his parade-ground bearing. He was wearing a top hat today, and whenever he took it in his hands, his wrist was forever repairing some blemish in the nap that only he could have been aware of.

Pickford made them all wait outside while he went first into the farmhouse. He treated the place with an air of ownership, and it was evident that he was up to something in there, for two or three minutes elapsed before he called some of them in by name.

'Constable Judson, you will take post outside. Can you remember the drill and signal I've taught you?'

'Sir.'

'Brunt—remove the manacles from the prisoner.'

The handcuffs were awkward. Brunt knew them immediately. They were a pair that every detective did his best to avoid when drawing equipment from the Derby office. He fumbled with a key that did not want to fit the mechanism. Ludlam came to his help, had the thing open in a single exploratory movement of sensitive fingers. Brunt noticed that he used his left hand; of course, he had to. Pickford looked on sourly.

'Pity you're not carrying a gun, Brunt. You could have got him to hold that for you, too. Bring him indoors.'

The room was stale, disrupted, unlived-in. Bagguley had taken himself off to lodge with a married sister off a cart track below the village. The smell was a mixture of the Bagguleys, of Mrs Bagguley's cooking, of the cumulative hungry history of the house—and a sickening aftermath of blood. Furniture had been moved about—the table pushed back and chairs shoved into unusable positions. The home had always had a face of inhospitability; now it was a house that loathed the human presence.

Neither Brunt nor Nadin had been informed of the circumstances in which the Bagguley woman had been found killed. Nor was it obvious why Pickford had brought Ludlam back for this obviously stage-managed visit. He suddenly made a movement—so sudden and pugnacious that it looked for a second as if he was going to hit Ludlam. Ludlam certainly thought so, for he took an involuntary half-step backwards—which gave Pickford great satisfaction, since he clearly thought that Ludlam was wilting under stress. But Ludlam did not twitch a hand either in defence or reprisal. And all that Pickford did was to draw out of his greatcoat pocket a small ball of screwed-up paper, which he threw down against the skirting-board, where it rolled under a chair.

'Pick it up!'

Ludlam acted without delay or reluctance, stooped and scrabbled for it—with his right hand, though that was insignificant. The retrieval required neither digital skill nor strength, and to have used his left hand would have involved a ludicrous contortion. He straightened himself up, and with a politeness that might possibly have been taken as provocative, offered the paper to the Inspector. Pickford turned impatiently away.

'Point proven, I think—in front of witnesses. You are not left-handed—you are ambidextrous.'

A ridiculous contention, as based on this biased and inadequate experiment. Brunt could not help looking at the Inspector's face. Who was he trying to convince? Himself? There was a masculinity about Pickford's expression: if it was manly to use eyebrows and chin solely for aggression; if it was masculine to cultivate military moustaches past active military age. Pickford had looked at Brunt like that over a misspelt word in a report. Brunt discovered—afresh—how much he hated Pickford. And it was not only for having become a top policeman without ever having been a policeman.

'If your manual skills are what you claim they are, you *would* have equal skills in both hands, wouldn't you?'

Nadin and Brunt waited as expressionless as they could make themselves for Ludlam's reply. But Pickford gave him no time.

'That's if you ever were a craftsman at all, and not just a radical *agent provocateur*—a rabble-rouser.'

There was evidently some chapter in Ludlam's history that Pickford had gone into—and not to Ludlam's advantage. Ludlam simply stared Pickford out—not with sardonic inner satisfaction, not with challenge—a plain, unemotional stare. Pickford passed in front of him and went and tapped three times on the window. Conscious histrionics: obviously the pre-arranged signal to Judson. They heard Judson's boots negotiating rubble in the yard, the creak of a hinge as he opened the door of one of the outhouses. Brunt wished he dared move over the necessary foot that would enable him to see what was happening. But it was best to do nothing that might draw himself to Pickford's attention.

Two pairs of feet crossed the flagstones, and then Judson threw the door open, holding his arm high for a woman to pass under it. Brunt had been expecting nothing exceptional. He was startled by the apparition that entered the room. It could so easily have been Molly Bagguley—black, shiny rags and a sacking apron that might actually have been hers. But she was splashed with red paint, fresh red, as if she were still bleeding from the neck. Brunt recognized Turner, a junior from the Derby office, his throat painted with an enormous crimson gash, with suitable splashes over cheeks, nostrils and eyebrows.

Nadin was looking at this creature with features devoid of expression. Pickford was staring bulbously, expectant. This was Pickford being at his most clever in public, believing no doubt that this stroke would be talked about in the chart-rooms of Derbyshire crime for ever. Did he so badly need to force a confession?

The apparition went and stood in front of Ludlam, leering into his face as if some cheapjack theatre were putting on *Macbeth* as a barnstorming melodrama. Then hands that could not possibly have been Molly Bagguley's shot out to Ludlam's shoulders, the eyes looked into Ludlam's from a short distance. The arms went round Ludlam's waist, and he was hugged tight into the black tatters.

Little else happened. Ludlam was forced back an inch or two by sheer overbalance of weight. But once he had found the right stance, he stood his ground. They all waited. A minute. A minute and a half. Then Pickford, resigned to failure, stepped forward and tapped the playactor's shoulder. Turner released Ludlam and stood back. Ludlam looked first briefly at Nadin, then briefly at Brunt, then with prolonged interest at Pickford. And then he began to laugh.

There was no touch of hysteria in it. It was the plain laughter of a man who has been shown something unex-pectedly comic—rather like an elderly gentleman who has caught a moment of forgotten childhood from the wooden benches of a circus. It was too much for Pickford.

'As I thought—not a shred of humanity—not a showing of remorse.'

Brunt had hated Pickford more or less at first sight, but he had never before realized how basically weak the man was. He suddenly caught sight of the mock Mrs Bagguley, now standing by, redundant and preposterous, looking nothing like what Pickford had wanted him to be.

'Get out of my sight, you stumbling jackass!'

Perhaps he genuinely thought it was Turner's fault that the act had failed.

'Put the cuffs back on him, Brunt—if you can. Judson—have my carriage brought up here.'

This time, Ludlam offered no assistance with the key.

'May I ask, Inspector Pickford—?'

'No, you may not ask. How can you think you are in a position to ask anything?'

'I am not, I think, to be kept *incommunicado* to my friends and advisers?'

'You will be treated entirely according to the law and to standing orders.'

'Then I ask for information about Mrs Eva Hargreaves.'

'You do not have to worry about her. And—not that it can be of any practical interest to you—she has asked that you should be kept away from her.'

'That's as may be. But I have the right to be told of her welfare—her whereabouts.'

'She is in good hands. Could not be better. She is in the Infirmary.'

'Infirmary? Do you mean Manchester?'

'Bakewell. In the sick quarters of the House of Industry. Where else?'

And it was then that Ludlam lost his self-control, as Pickford had been trying to make him do from the outset. His anger shook Brunt's wrist and arm.

'Inspector Pickford—when a woman's life has been what Eva's has been, when she is ending her days in the wrecked stage she has reached—can the state find no better comfort for her than—?'

'Take him outside, Brunt. I refuse to let him use me as an ear-trumpet for political agitation.'

So they stepped among the rubbish of the yard, to await the carriage that was already coming along the approach lane. Ludlam was laboriously transferred to the wrist of one of Pickford's waiting minions. He had calmed down again

now, did not catch either Brunt's or Nadin's eye. For the final
scene of the morning, Pickford took Nadin and Brunt to one
side.

'I am parting you two. You're no good for each other, and
even less use to the Force. You, Nadin—you did no sort of job
on that fishing-gear theft up in Hartington. It's turning into a
regular traffic. Now there's a Hardy rod reported missing at
Tissington, and God knows what from the Dog and Par-
tridge at Thorpe. Get on over there, and don't show your face
again until you've retrieved every last inch of line.'

'Very good.'

No *sir*. But otherwise Nadin seemed quite unmoved.

'And you. Brunt—get down to Darley Dale. This Pilkington woman, the one you reported as believed to have left the
country: she's making a nuisance of herself in and around an
old people's nursing home. Make sure she commits an
offence this time—and make sure you nail it on her.'

CHAPTER 11

Brunt was never at his happiest as far downstream as Darley
Dale. Himself an immigrant from a working street in a
coal-mining town in the north-east of the county, there was
something in the primeval wastes of the Peak that spoke to
him of life in the early days of Creation. Once the Wye had
become the Derwent, having tumbled several hundred feet
from its source, it had widened and begun to meander
through cress beds and lush meadows. To Brunt this was a
countryside too easygoing, too fertile, and occupied by a race
too well provided for, too sheltered, too unpressed. South of
Chatsworth, he never could resist the fancy that he was being
looked down on.

He had no difficulty in locating Amelia Pilkington. She
was staying at the Reapers Hotel, in itself no mean feat for an

unmarried woman, not yet old, travelling alone at the zenith of the century's hypocritical years. But Amelia Pilkington had not arrived where she had—including time living on the hospitality of the state—without acquiring the short-term knack of gaining the sympathy of strangers.

In Darley Dale she was not Amelia Pilkington. In Buxton she had been a fashionable lady of the colonnades and the Pump Room, in a wide-brimmed hat set slightly askew with a vestigial lavender veil. Her sleeves had been puffed out and her half-dozen petticoats had imparted a swirl to her skirt that had had retired Crimean majors cricking their necks. That Sir William Palfreyman had been the one allowed to win had been a credit, not only to her own staff-work, but also to previous inquiries made by her male accomplice, in whose company Buxton had not been allowed to see her.

In Darley Dale she was still Amelia, but Carstairs, whose hair was beginning to show enough salting of grey to absolve her from any initial label of flightiness. She was wearing blouse and skirt in a sober and less than imperial purple, and neat but stout boots, admirable in a town-lady who had equipped herself realistically for a fortnight in the country.

She had given it out that she was staying locally in order to give attention to a cousin a generation removed, at present on the brink of decline in The Alders. This was a claim that no one could check on first hearing, and indeed it seemed so naively sincere that only the likes of Pickford, Nadin or Brunt would have seen any need to have to check it at all. And after the first few days, all but the hardened sceptics would have been happy with their checking. The experienced intelligence work of her accomplice had already picked out a potentially profitable cousin. She had already made contact with him—when, with three others, he was being taken for a quarter-mile afternoon walk by an elderly nurse. He was a man quick on the uptake, despite some diminishing capacities, and latched quickly on to the convenience of letting her be known as a cousin. The village, The Reapers, and even the staff of The Alders, had naturally believed that Amelia Carstairs represented a wing of the family who were hostile to those who had had the old man put out to care.

All of this Brunt learned without undue exertion. He already knew The Alders. It was not an establishment known for the innovations of its medical consultants, nor for the adventurousness of its gastronomy. But it was above the threshold on which it could be accused of actual meanness or provable negligence. It was discreet, it kept out of the news, and it had tasteful surrounds which impressed visitors, especially from May to September. Outside those months, there were in any case relatively few visitors.

Amelia Carstairs's new cousin gave Brunt no trouble. The indigenous population of Darley Dale knew only a few legendary titbits about the residents at The Alders: that one had been a general, another a painter, and so on. Otherwise there were gaps, social, intellectual and one might almost say tribal between the village and the nursing home. Brunt therefore had to give his mind to forming a liaison with someone on the staff of The Alders who might be persuaded to prattle about the inmates,

He found such a contact in the shape—perhaps it would be more courteous to say figure—of a trainee under-cook, by name Fanny Metcalfe, whom he met by a carefully contrived coincidence in a lane as she came back from posting a letter. It is a further coincidence that this young woman was destined to become Mrs Brunt, but that development does not matter to this story, except in so far as the inclinations of both parties facilitated Brunt's access to the Home. And since that powerful elder stateswoman, Cook herself, had a weepy eye for romance, and seemed to approve of him, his way in and out was almost free of obstacles.

But he was restless whenever the image of George Ludlam came into his mind. There was a heart-sinking dearth of information. Ludlam appeared twice before the Derby justices and was twice remanded for a week in custody, the second time at the request of his own lawyer, who needed time for marshalling his defence. From Jimmy Nadin there came no news at all. Either he was deeply involved in his robbers' den of fishing-rods, or he was ignoring orders altogether and had vanished back to the routines that he preferred.

Then Brunt was bidden to the Derby headquarters, and when he was told that he was to stand by for interview with Pickford, he began to wonder what other walks of life might be open to him—always provided that they would not take him too far away from the kitchens at Darley Dale. But Pickford was not in unduly abusive mood. He might already be bathing in the forthcoming triumph of his swift and clever solution of the Ludlam case.

'This Pilkington woman, Brunt. You've put nothing on paper for a week. Are you wasting your time?'

'No, sir. I will write an interim report while I am here. I could summarize it for you now, sir.'

'Do that, Brunt. It will save my having to labour through your subordinate clauses.'

'Well, sir, she has attached herself to a Mr Reginald Burdell, younger member of a family of small private bankers in London. When I say younger member, I refer to his family standing. He is actually seventy-three—'

'Yes, yes—get on, Brunt.'

'There seems to have been a certain slackness among the nursing-home staff who escort Burdell on his constitutionals. And I have heard it said in The Alders that he is quite lavish with gratuities. Miss Carstairs, as she is now calling herself, seems to have flattered him into thinking that she has a soft spot for his company.'

'Yes. That's the target in view. But what does she actually want from him?'

'I understand, sir—'

Brunt understood it because Reginald Burdell had in

senile excitement discussed it with a fellow patient, who had mentioned it to a gossiping nurse, who had carried it down to the kitchen.

'That she has talked to him about the money that she is trying to save so that her younger sister can have a vital operation. It can be performed only by a surgeon at the University of Bonn. Bonn is in Rhenish Prussia, sir.'

'That sounds like Miss Pilkington. Is Burdell taking the bait?'

'Up to now he seems a trifle uncertain, sir. He seems to develop a certain hardness of hearing whenever she broaches the topic.'

'Her next move, Brunt, will be to tell him that she is going to have to leave Darley Dale. This will depress him. Shortly after that, she will have him.'

'I'm sure she will, sir.'

'So make sure that you then have her—the moment money passes. You're sure of your source?'

Brunt tried to picture Fanny Metcalfe, and realized how basically unsure he still was of her.

'As sure as I think one can ever be, sir.'

'Don't waver, Brunt. Finger on the trigger's one thing. Guts to pull it's quite another. I've known men—'

But he seemed to think, suddenly, that it was time he restored himself to his proper position.

'You *are* wavering, Brunt.'

'I think not, sir.'

'As useless as udders on a bull, you and Nadin were, that morning at Litton.'

Brunt waited.

'Best thing I ever did, Brunt, getting Nadin off your back. At least, I'll begin to think so when Miss Pilkington is shaking the bars.'

On principle, he looked at Brunt as he had looked at Ludlam at Starve-Acre.

Brunt returned to Darley Dale, and ran headlong into

Amelia Carstairs. Thus far he had managed to avoid her tracks. It had been fortuitously easy to do this, since she was generally involved with Mr Reginald Burdell at those hours when Fanny could most easily be spared from the kitchen. When Fanny had afternoon tea to prepare, Brunt was often allowed to hang about near her, waiting for a cup; and at that time Amelia, the accepted cousin, was often upstairs in the residents' sitting-room.

But this afternoon, arriving back from Derby, Brunt was hurrying back to The Alders by the quickest and most exposed route. And he met Amelia face to face.

She, of course, knew him. There had been no need to conceal himself in Buxton, while Nadin was openly torment-ing her. She saw no point now in trying to dissimulate.

'Oh, my God, not you!' she said.

And then she started to cry.

'Mr Brunt—tell me. Is that other man with you? That Sergeant Nadin?'

'No. He's a long way away.'

'Is there somewhere we can go and talk, Mr Brunt?'

She seized Brunt's arm above the wrist. He caught a whiff of the scent that set old men tottering. She had a pink bloom on her cheek, and her cheek was near to his face. He could feel the warmth of her, inches away. It was the sort of proximity that he was still afraid to dare with Fanny Met-calfe.

'I know—let's go down to the church. All visitors to Darley Dale do that.'

She was now gripping him tight, walking him down the hill.

'I just have to talk to you, Mr Brunt. It's all so unfair. How much are they paying you to stay on my heels? A pound a week and your boot leather—and a stingy enough allowance for that?'

She pushed open the lychgate, and there was an elderly group looking at the inscriptions on tombs. While they were in earshot, Amelia Pilkington spoke in a loud voice for their benefit.

'Isn't it marvellous to think that that yew-tree provided the bow-shanks for Agincourt? I love history.'

She knew her way round that church and its yard. When she came to a new neighbourhood as a knowledgeable visitor, she always made sure that she lived up to her image. She showed Brunt the tomb of Sir John de Darley. And once they were shielded from the public view, she took his arm agai..

'Mr Brunt, did Sergeant Nadin tell you to follow me here? I only came here to rest. I had such a dreadful time in Buxton. Your horrible sergeant assumed that if I made friends with a gentle old man, I must be up to no good—Oh, I know, Mr Brunt, I've done wrong in my time. But has it been so very, very wrong? Somehow, old people like me. They appear to take to me. If I have brought them a little pleasure and happiness—a little something to live for in their last few months—what am I to do if they offer me little presents?'

She raised her eyes searchingly into his. Brunt almost quailed before the intensity of the appeal.

'Even here, where, as I say, I came for a few quiet weeks to be out of harm's way, I can't help meeting a poor old gentleman who says he likes my company so much that he pleads with me never to go away. What am I to do, Mr Brunt?'

Brunt knew well enough what she was going to do. He had had Mr Reginald Burdell pointed out to him in The Alders. He was a well-made, dapper, grey-haired man who wore a quilted smoking-jacket most of the time indoors—and who lived now for the fun of intriguing his friends in the Home with supposition about his new lady-friend. Brunt had had a memorandum on him from one of Pickford's clerks. Whatever one did as a junior partner in a private bank, Burdell had come to the end of it; maybe he had been too conservative for end-of-century finance. His wife had died giving stillbirth while she was a young woman. In his sixties he had had an illness that had been messy and expensive. They had persuaded him to come here to convalesce. He had convalesced, was too tired to want to face any new set of circumstances. A relative—to whom he was totally indifferent—came to see him twice a year.

The bulk of his income was interest on closely-tied shares in the family holding. Let him try to touch those, and there would be consternation in a corner of the City—and influential pressure for action, swift and final. But it was presumed that he had something put aside to assure his independence, some private account to which his access was personal.

Amelia had charmed him. She had become part of his day—walks in the grounds, tea in corners of the brocaded sitting-room. Perhaps he thought she was truly enchanted by him—he who had enchanted no one for years. Perhaps she reminded him of vigours that he once possessed: perhaps in secret moments he even thought of regaining those vigours. He was too shrewd a man not partly to suspect her motives. Whence otherwise his comic talk to his friends about pretending to be deaf when she touched on certain subjects? But a relic of the old shrewdness was not enough to fight off the other tumults. There was no limit to which Amelia would not go in her end-game. Certainly she would soon announce that she would have to leave Darley Dale. She would harp with great skill on the void she was leaving behind her. Burdell, finally not caring whether he was being duped or not—because, he would tell himself, he could afford it—would bribe her to stay. There would be a letter to post: instructions to his bankers. She would take the draft and go.

Because patient though Amelia was, talented companion of the aged and the solitary, she had her limitations. There was a point at which she became bored by present company. It was at times like that that her concentration diminished. Once or twice in the past she had become careless—and had found herself under arrest. Moreover, Nadin believed that she was being managed by a man, almost always a lap or two ahead of her on the circuit, and she would surely like to catch sight of him from time to time—even if only to hear about the next lucrative situation he had found for her.

'So do tell me you're not going to drive me away from here, Mr Brunt.'

A heartfelt appeal: she truly believed that she could do with Brunt what she wanted. Brunt was uneasy, embarrassed—but fundamentally not to be shaken. Amelia Whatever-she-cared-to-call-herself did make mistakes. They had made inroads in her freedom before now.

'Why should I drive you away? As long as you are behaving yourself—'

'Oh, Mr Brunt—'

The glint of gratitude, the underlying hint that if he behaved himself too, he might be surprised at some of the things she would do for him.

'As a matter of fact,' Brunt said, 'it isn't exactly business that brings me to Darley Dale.'

'No?'

'Though in my walk of life, it's pretty easy to find business of some sort or other wherever I want to be.'

'You're deeper than you look, if I may say so, Mr Brunt. Then what—?'

Then she correctly interpreted his coy look.

'Oh, how lovely—who is she, Mr Brunt?'

'As a matter of fact, it hasn't quite reached the stage at which I ought to be talking about her.'

'Oh, Mr Brunt—if there's anything I can do to help—'

They came out of the churchyard and Brunt suddenly winced with grit in his eye, so that they had to stand still while Amelia, vertiginously close and perfumed, did her best to remove it with a corner of delicate handkerchief. At least he had managed to keep her back towards the direction in which she had almost turned. He had just caught sight of

Jimmy Nadin, looking more than ever like a round-shouldered little monkey, with absurdly big ears and round, incredulous eyes.

Brunt said he would walk Miss Carstairs back to her hotel, which would give Nadin a chance to make himself scarce—if only the man used his wits. And when Brunt at last dared look back over his shoulder, Nadin had gone.

CHAPTER 12

Nadin had an encyclopædic knowledge of the taprooms of Derbyshire, especially those in which discreet conversations were possible.

'So how's Amelia?'

Brunt brought him up to date.

'Critical,' Nadin said. 'That's if you really want to pull her in this time.'

I think I shall have to. Pickford—'

'Giving Pickford his way now, are we? It's probably no bad thing to do something he wants, once in a while. But you're not going around thinking you've fooled Amelia, are you?'

Brunt had omitted to say anything about Fanny Metcalfe, so one of the stoutest props to his story was missing.

'I rather believe Miss Carstairs thinks I'm a bit of an ass,' Brunt said.

Nadin held back his head in a way that he had, drawing his chin in almost to his Adam's apple.

'By God, Tom, if you can keep that up for the rest of your days, you're a made man.'

'No, seriously—'

'Yes, well, no—seriously—you know what Amelia's going to do now, don't you? She's going to have to act fast. And you've got to act fast too. She'll threaten to leave here. She's going to have to break poor old Reggie's heart. She's got to push him over the brink within the next forty-eight hours, sooner if she can, and get her hands on the draft or whatever. And it's going to help your case no end if you can find it on her. And get a statement out of Reggie—which might mean reading him a firm lecture on the duties of the citizen. Because when he realizes what his relations are going to read in the newspapers about him—oh, you're going to have your work cut out, Tom Brunt.'

'I can see that.'

In fact, until now Brunt had not seen it so clearly. His anxiety showed.

'Like me to stay in the offing?'

But Brunt had already caught a glimpse of himself managing this.

'We're not supposed to be working together.'

'Oh, Tom—are you turning me down? Listen, lad, that's only what Pickford *said*. If we went about doing all Pickford said, we might as well stay at home with our pipes on and our feet on the mantelpiece. Success, that's what we need. We succeed—and Pickford will swear he put us on the job together.'

'And if we fail?'

'Pickford will say nasty things. You're too easily hurt, Tom. Besides, it isn't this case that interests us, is it?'

'Well, no—but I haven't heard a thing about—'

'That's what I came here to talk about. I was hoping you'd fancy a trip up to Bakewell.'

'Eva Hargreaves?'

'I'm afraid she's taken a dislike to me. Not in fact a very easy woman. I can see what George Ludlam was up against when they were kids.'

'I haven't heard any news at all about Ludlam.'

'Oh, Pickford's got him well and truly trussed—so he thinks. And unless someone can get Eva Hargreaves to talk, say what she saw and heard that morning—'

'Do you think you could start on page one, Jimmy?'

Nadin took a large pull at his pewter and passed it up to be refilled.

'The day Molly Bagguley was killed, George Ludlam went up to Starve-Acre to see Eva Hargreaves. That was Annie Barker's doing. She knows everything, and she knew that Molly was going to Chapel-en-le-Frith on the carrier's wagon, to do a bit of extra shopping, having been given money to spend on Mrs Hargreaves. And Ben Bagguley was going over to Eyam with a cartload of furniture to sell. We don't need to be told where that had come from, do we?'

Brunt was thinking that if Nadin were just a shade smaller, he would look very well in a green jacket and red fez—an organ-grinder's monkey to the T.

'Well, Ben went to Eyam, and there's a witness there, a dealer in the same sort of junk as himself, who has deposed to that. And Molly set off in the direction of Chapel-en-le-Frith, but Bert Potter broke an axle just before the Peak Forest crossroads, so Molly and two or three others cut their losses and came home on foot. Those two or three others all saw her go back to Starve-Acre. They don't carry watches, that lot, but it's reasonable to fix it at about a quarter to ten.'

Nadin tackled ear-wax with an irritable little finger.

'You mean,' Brunt said, 'that Eva Hargreaves had been left alone in the house?'

'I don't see we can croak about that. Doc Collins had been in twice to see her, and she was somewhat better, according to him. Confused in her head about some things, but she could get to the commode and such-like. Well, by now it's an open secret in Litton that George Ludlam's hidden away in the Cordwainers'. He's had one or two people in to see him, sent for privately by Annie, because he's started probing into the other two Bagguley cases—Nell Merridew, Isaac Slack—collecting anything he can get his ears to. He means to get the case against the Bagguleys that I couldn't. And Jack Judson's taking good care he doesn't hear what's going on. All the same, Annie doesn't think Ludlam had better tempt Providence by walking up the Litton street in broad daylight, so she fixes a ride for him. She has a brewer's delivery that morning and she arranges for Ludlam to get a lift up to Starve-Acre covered with sacks on the dray. What the hell a brewer's dray is supposed to be going up to Starve-Acre for, I don't know. But you can get away with most things in Litton village, if Litton village is with you.

'Annie Barker has told Ludlam where the Bagguleys leave the key when they're both out. I've told you—she knows everything. It's remarkable in a woman who never goes further than the end of her own yard. Under the water-butt, under a bit of slate. Ludlam fumbles about, can't find it—witness: the brewer's drayman. It's all the world against Ludlam, now the flood's over the crest. He tries the door, finds he can walk in. Walks in. There's Molly Bagguley lying on her face, blood everywhere. Ludlam behaves stupidly, not sure she's dead, he says, so he bends over to pick her up, whereupon her head all but comes off, cut through practically to the spinal column. Enter Tommy Lamp-oil, who's just had a row with the brewer's drayman for being in his way. Tommy goes down for Judson. Judson has no choice of immediate action.'

'And Ludlam still hadn't got to see Eva Hargreaves?'

'Eva Hargreaves isn't the easiest cog in the works. That's why I want you to go to try to have a word with her. She's taken exception to me.'

'Happen she'll take exception to me too.'

'If she does, it won't help Ludlam. Dr Collins could, if Pickford would listen to him. When Collins looked at her body, he said—and you wouldn't have to be a doctor to see it for yourself—that Mrs Bagguley had had her throat slashed from behind, and that by a right-handed man. Put yourself in the position, Tom—you're right-handed. You want to kill somebody from behind, you slash from your left to your right. Mrs Bagguley was slashed from right to left. You can tell that from the lie of the top layer of flesh, as well as from the lop-sided depth of the cut. Hence that pathetic business of Pickford's, trying to prove that Ludlam had equal use in both hands. Ludlam's been a craftsman—in wrought-iron, as it turns out—a master craftsman who needed strength as well as precision. It's when he gets this sort of clever notion into his head that Pickford takes leave of his sense of reality. Remember Ludlam's gesture, when he was haranguing us in Annie Barker's sitting-room? Left fist into right palm. That settles him as right-handed for me. That could go a long way to letting him out of the killing. His lawyer will be taking up court time on it. It would do me good to see Pickford come unstuck over it: but there's no banking on that. If the jury don't happen to like Ludlam, they'll like Pickford.'

'And what's been your trouble with Eva Hargreaves?'

'A difficult woman. That's why I want you to have a go at her.'

'What makes you think I'd do better than you did?'

'I think she might prefer your brand of—'

Nadin could not think of a word that Brunt might not find offensive.

'I think she might prefer you,' he said limply. 'She's not a nice woman. And when all's said and done, why the hell should she be? Remember the picture Ludlam painted: a hard-faced little Cockney sparrow, who'd survived Pancras Workhouse, Lowdham and Litton—and God knows what before the London Poor Law picked her up asleep on somebody's area steps. Eva Hargreaves doesn't trust anyone. And if it comes to that, do you and I?'

Nadin enlarged further on Eva the child, speculating on what Ludlam had told them. It was the story of impudence that would not allow itself to be crushed. She had been a strident leader among the girls. She had had cronies, but they were scarcely friends. Friendship implied a two-way traffic in affection and support. Eva must so often nearly have gone under that she was never on anyone's side but her own. She did sometimes leave her senses—boil over—as when she got herself punished under the machinery. Ludlam had told them how she had stood up to that. He had not been there to report how she had behaved when she returned to the mill. But there were one or two in Litton who remembered.

Needham had not brought her in from her convalescence until the afternoon shift. She had come into the mill swinging her crooked and badly set leg out at a provocative angle, had stood for a few seconds taking in anything that had changed, any faces that were new. Anyone who had come to Needham's mill later than she had was beneath her consideration. She saw a girl who was strange to her working at the bank of spindles that she regarded as hers. She strode—hardly *strode*—launched herself with her leg swinging sideways, barged the girl with her shoulder.

'My place!'

And she took possession of it at once. And not everyone at the mill was of the same calibre as Billy Orgill and Ned Woodward. There was a good deal of pity for the London kids, though it had to remain merely verbal, if jobs were to be kept. But there were a few who were prepared to take risks, even sacrifice a few pennies, to alleviate the lot of someone whose position was scandalous. One who did his best in a small way was Michael Hargreaves from the village, who worked in the mill as a blacksmith, forging spare parts for the machinery and shoeing Needham's stable of wagon-horses. If a child had a ha'penny to spend, earned perhaps for forgoing his dinner—or pilfered from someone else who had—it was always safe to creep round the back of the smithy and give Hargreaves a commission: a baked custard tart, or a pasty, which he would bring down to work with him the next morning.

Eva was a good customer of Hargreaves. She was popular with the smith because of her injury, and she sometimes came in with orders costing as much as five ha'pennies. No one believed she was honest—but no one thought of accusing her. She had a rancorous manner, and people preferred not to tangle with it. They forgave her for all sorts of things because of her leg, and she knew how to exploit it.

'It seems funny,' Brunt said, 'that Ludlam should have been bemused by someone so different from himself.'

'Attraction of opposites.'

'And he's remained loyal to her over all these years?'

'Loyal, perhaps—but no longer infatuated. He feels—I expect he feels it still in his cell—that somebody owes her something. She's a sort of symbol to him of those that went under.'

A couple of years after her accident, Needham had closed the mill for Good Friday. It was a gesture not so much of religion as of pretence. Needham was a friend of the priest at Tideswell—and talk of new Factory Acts was in the air. Hot cross buns were promised: but they were cynical about these in the Apprentices' House. Eva gave her own order in at the forge. And since the smith was not coming to work in the morning, he sent his son Ned, a strapping stone-worker of eighteen, who came down with a basket.

Eva was capable of falling in love—and that got her out of the mill. Young Hargreaves was often down to see her. Some believed that Needham might lean on his rights under her so-called indenture and make things difficult. In fact, he was not sorry to be rid of the figure with the grotesque gait whose accident might still blow back in his face. He even gave a wedding-party for the workers: dancing to a fiddle and drum, an extra oatcake each—and an hour's relaxation of discipline that led to more fighting than fun.

Ned Hargreaves adored Eva—and did a lot for her. He was patient. It was said that it took him ten years to tame her. She made no village friends in her life. She had to be taught the first elements of housekeeping. In the early years, before she learned a little civilization, he did a lot of compensation for petty thefts—until she began to learn what people would not stand for. She was a quarrelsome partner—but when Ned died, she knew what he had meant to her. She became more than ever a recluse. It was Tommy Lamp-oil who first discovered how ill she was—a bout of bronchitis. And that was where the Bagguleys had stepped in.

'And how's she reacting to Bakewell Workhouse?' Brunt asked.

'Go and see, lad.'

'And how did you get on with all that fishing-gear?'

'I haven't had time to get over to Hartington yet.'

CHAPTER 13

One story remained to be told: the history of George Ludlam over the fifty years that had passed between his escape from Needham's mill and Brunt's meeting with him on the north-bound Midland train.

Ludlam had told it to Annie Barker, during the long hours that they had spent together while she was hiding him in the Cordwainers' Arms, and Nadin unfolded it to Brunt now. There was no doubting that Annie was far gone in her admiration for Ludlam—the sort of reason-bursting adoration that had not happened to Annie since the single, committed love of her youth. It was a relationship that called forth a grotesque image: the tall, preserved, dignified, erstwhile taciturn enigma—and the obese, rotund, degenerating, mock-bad-tempered old woman. But Nadin waved that chain of thought to one side. Annie was too savage a realist to expect anything of this friendship. It was just that she was not beyond indulging herself in the rosiness of the rolling moment.

The boy Ludlam had come out through fields on to the top road that leads down from Litton to the southern exit of the dale at the Cressbrook end. But he had been out of the mill grounds so infrequently that he was in no position to know much of local topography. He was aware, he said, of a poetical sense of freedom, a gratitude for the night about him—and a conviction that every yard he could stagger ahead was taking him farther from Needham. But his euphoria was short-lived. He was weak and in pain from his last thrashing. The night was too cold for him, and too impenetrable. When he found his feet carrying him steadily downhill, he began to fear that in his ignorance he was wandering in a circle that would suddenly plunge him back within Needham's precincts. He was beyond reasonable self-direction. And when he heard double footsteps behind him, quickening as they drew near to his heels, he had only one interpretation: that it was a posse of Needham's foremen, or, equally bad, local inhabitants who had heard him pass in the dark and were greedy for the five shillings that might be earned for returning him to the mill.

Like a locomotive fireman who throws coal on to a fire that is already straining the rivets of the boiler, Ludlam tried to thrust extra speed into himself. The result was a physical experience new to him. He was accustomed to the struggle to choke pain out of his consciousness. He could walk until a stitch in his side vanished into oblivion. But what was happening now was a drainage of blood from his brain, a creeping uselessness that took his limbs out of his control. He was only fifteen, Nadin reminded Brunt—undernourished, overdriven, corporally cut to pieces. He fainted—fell forward on his face and knees in the long, wet grass at the side of the road. He thought he was dying. He was aware of figures bending over him. He tried to roll over to avoid the kick in the ribs that he expected. But he did not remain conscious to know whether it materialized or not.

His memory of the next few hours was like a scrapbook flicked against the thumb. He was being helped to stumble along the road by a strong arm about both shoulders. There was an imperative knocking at a door, a face looking out over

a storm-lantern, angry and perplexed at first, dissolving into
concern when a woman in a nightcap saw the weals across
his back. Bed, in an attic all rafters and coffers; someone
kindling fire in a hearth. A platter was brought to him by the
woman of last night—anxious, outraged and encouraging all
in the same moment—and convinced that the proper treatment for a maltreated adolescent boy was three rashers of
ham, half an inch thick, with four fried eggs. She was
disturbed when he could not face up to it. Within a week he
was eating all that she could put before him.

He had been picked up on the road by a couple called
Gladwin. But Henry Gladwin had gone on ahead, on some
business about which George Ludlam was not clear. When
Ludlam did meet him, he was a man nearing forty, dusty and
creased from the road, but nevertheless steady-headed and
holding himself straight-backed. Gladwin's wife, who had
stayed behind with young George in the farmhouse where
she had pleaded for help for him last night, was some five
years younger than her husband. She had long periods of
silence. When she did talk, it was because she had something
to say, and she said it with a loving Lancashire burr, a dialect
that Ludlam had heard from some of the imported cotton-
workers at Litton.

When Gladwin returned, the first thing that he announced
about himself was that he was a fighting man, always had
been. He was infuriated by what Ludlam had told them
about Needham, and his instinct was to go back to the
Justices and make a fighting job of it this time. His wife did
not give her opinion until she was asked, and then she was for
pushing on out of harm's way. There was no question, it
seemed, but that Ludlam was to remain in their company.
Faced with opposing opinions, the man turned to Ludlam
and asked him for his. George Ludlam was in favour of
putting distance between themselves and Litton.

'Yet you look to me as if you've always fought back until
now,' Henry Gladwin said.

'But, Henry, you know that you've also to find work,' his wife said. 'Empty pockets and famished bellies never fought for justice.'

The Gladwins were trades unionists—at least, Henry was, and Mary Anne was his woman. He was of the Fine Metal Workers and Allied Trades, one of the first facts that George Ludlam learned about him, for the man proudly showed him a membership card, with a handsomely printed escutcheon showing medieval craft-workers with the tools of their trade. Henry Gladwin was a worker in wrought-iron.

There was a system in operation at the time whereby paid-up and accredited craftsmen who were out of work could wander the country, getting board and frugal subsistence at inns designated as Union centres, these charitable expenses being paid for by a levy on all members. Should the unemployed man come to a place where there was a vacancy in his calling, then he was allowed to take it on a roster arrangement, provided that that meant no unfairness to local workers.

The Gladwins had to tell lies about George Ludlam, but they did this with ease of conscience. They had no papers for him, so he became Mary Anne Gladwin's sister's son, who had lost both parents in a weaving-shed disaster in Chorley: which strained no man's belief. In that role he was accepted at Chesterfield, where they were given bread, cheese and beer—and told that the town had more Fine Metal Workers on the road than there were at the forges. Later, when Gladwin was temporarily in work and putting in late-night overtime, he had papers counterfeited by an easy going printer—and Ludlam began to live an existence without explanations.

There was a month's work for Gladwin at Worksop, and though there was no opening in an apprenticeship for Ludlam, he was allowed into the shop, where he watched basic processes and plunged in at every chance to try his own hand.

Then they had to move on: Doncaster, Rotherham, Thorne: there were many more nights at Union inns. It was a bad time for wrought-iron workers. The age they lived in was demanding multi-production. Even heating conduits in church floors were being covered by cast-iron tracery. The man who slowly produced the work of his hands was lucky if his small master was still getting commissions.

For eight or nine months the three of them tramped, hoped, would settle for a week, then tramp on. Sometimes George Ludlam found menial odd-jobbing, from which he could contribute to the family purse. Henry Gladwin began to despair. He had heard that things were better in Prussia, and that their Union brothers on the North German Plain were not averse to honest travellers. They had wandered within striking distance of the coast. From Goole they sailed steerage to Hamburg, a foul crossing that took all of two days, and emptied their bellies of the last aching heave of bile.

'Ludlam was not impressed by the Prussian Union movement,' Nadin said. 'It lacked the planning and the solid brotherhood of its English counterpart. There were too many Grand Duchies and Principalities where they were satisfied with their own way of doing things. But there was still patronage of fine arts. Ludlam became parted from the Gladwins when he was taken on by an old man in a small town in Mark Brandenburg.'

He served his time at that forge and the old man pleaded with him to stay. But Ludlam—who had truly found his métier—wanted to advance to something more celebrated than provincial balconies and grilles for ground-floor windows. He moved away on a true journeyman stage, passing from master to master, making and outgrowing friendships, adding to his skills, engendering new ideas and ambitions.

'No woman?' Brunt asked.

'If there was, he didn't tell Annie Barker about her.'

Ludlam arrived in a free city, seat of an autonomic *Graf*.

They were reconstructing their cathedral.

'He told Annie that he always looked on it as his cathedral, because everything that men's hands had put into it was part of its soul. He and Annie Barker must have had some fairly far-reaching conversations.'

And George Ludlam's rood-screen was distinguished enough to qualify as his masterpiece. The *Gewerkschaft* recognized him as a master, and with his accumulated savings— he had spent very little on himself, and had none of the surprise expenses of a family—he set himself up in a small way.

'And actually,' Jimmy Nadin said. 'I have had confirmation of all this from an unexpected source. There are a couple of Germans in the Buxton Gardens Orchestra. I talked to a man called Franz Heining—a beautiful violinist. And he knows both the church and the rood-screen. He had heard it said that it was made by an Englishman. Small world, isn't it?'

Ludlam had gone on to win one guaranteed assignment after another. He had become the favourite craftsman of a cultural *Verein* that was touching up the fussy rococo churches of Württemberg and Baden. But Ludlam was becoming uneasy.

'This is a vulgar age,' he had told Annie Barker. 'It is an age that worships bigness for its own sake Prussia may have entered the industrial field later than us, but they are developing fast. Their Chancellor has eaten up the autonomous states. His wars—Denmark, then France—'

It was within a year of the end of the Franco-Prussian conflict that Ludlam finally decided to break with the land in which he had made his name. He had come home, with no plans more specific than to satisfy nostalgic curiosity. It was scarcely a hunger for the past: a mere titillation of taste-buds. He had bought a map to see how the railway pioneers had dealt with the prohibitive valleys been Monsal and Miller's Dales. The last person he had ever expected to find alive and almost *in situ* was Eva Hargreaves.

'Small world, isn't it?' Nadin asked again.

'It is if you turn back on yourself,' Brunt said.

CHAPTER 14

Bakewell Workhouse was an univiting stone building dating from the 1840s. Nineteenth-century houses of industry were never intended to be inviting places. The destitute had to be provided for—but not as an encouragement to the unwilling. The discipline had to be explicit: the 'casuals' could be positively dangerous. They were called houses of industry because work of a sort, sometimes futile, had to be done in payment for charity received. There were insensitive practices, for example the separation of married couples and families. But underneath the faults of the system, seams of kindness and sympathy could exist—even love of one person for another.

Brunt had been in the Bakewell Union once before, which saved time when he sought entry now. The Infirmary was new to him. The women's ward was a long room on the ground floor, accommodating some forty patients in beds almost as close foot to foot as they were side by side. Every window was barred—a fascinating forethought. Would anyone fortunate enough to be outside put himself to the trouble of trying to break in? Certainly all those within were too frail and sapped of will ever to think of breaking out.

The nurse on duty was an Irish girl, who had put her youth behind her and showed no signs of wishing to preserve it. She was willing enough in a lackadaisical way, wearing the flatness of her brogue like a hallmark, and spreading about her an acrid indictment of her personal hygiene. But she grasped Brunt's identity, admissibility and purpose in one mental step, and led him at once to Eva Hargreaves's bed.

This was roughly in the middle of the room, and she was sitting up in it looking spare, wiry and at odds with the world. Whoever had combed her hair—it may not have been that morning—had achieved two partings that did not come together. Her cheeks were fallen in. She had no teeth and her eyes had in them a light which suggested that she was in no mind to accept everything she saw.

'Nobody's had a lot of sleep since she came here,' Bridget Murphy said.

'She's not made friends with anyone?'

'I don't think she'd know what to do with a friend if she had one.'

There were women lying on their backs looking at the ceiling, women sitting up in their beds looking at nothing, women whose minds had gone, women, in some cases, whose minds at the height of their powers had never amounted to much. Somewhere towards the farther end of the ward a woman was crying, a long, unpunctuated snivel. Another was picking at something that did not exist on the folded-down sheet in front of her: hallucinations, chimera, disconnected incidents from deprived pasts, conversations from bed to bed that scarcely overlapped. Most pathetic of all was the idleness. Nobody had anything to do. Eyes were glazed from months of looking at what was not worth seeing.

And Eva Hargreaves? Her eyes were not glazed yet, perhaps because she had not been here long enough. What, beyond hating, was going on behind those eyes? And what was she hating? How much continuous thought was going on inside that head? Had her highest moment been as a child of nine or ten, the conscious leader? God knows, she could have led no one anywhere, but hers was the gutter shrillness that the others had responded to. Had she seen her leadership threatened when the boy Ludlam had arrived with a later draft at the mill; because George Ludlam had always had ideas; because somewhere in George Ludlam's blood and humours there was a hereditary touch of decency? Was this what Eva, gutter-sharp and gutter-unforgiving, had seen and most resented? She must have known how young Ludlam longed for and needed her approval. She must have resolved at sight that he should never have it. It was only in such decisions that power existed at Needham's mill.

Nurse Murphy brought up a bare wooden chair and Brunt sat down by the bed.

'Good morning, Mrs Hargreaves. I hope they're treating you well.'

'I want to go home,' she said

'I'm afraid that's not possible just now. Mrs Bagguley has had an accident.'

'Accident!'

Did she know what had happened? That she had had bronchitis? That the poisons from her lungs had clouded her brain, that no one else in the village would have waited on her, and that if the Bagguleys had not carried her up to Starve-Acre she would very shortly have died in her own cottage?

'Mrs Hargreaves, you say it was no accident. Do you *know* what happened to Molly Bagguley?'

'You'd like to know, wouldn't you?'

'Mrs Hargreaves, did you get out of bed that morning? Did you go to the window?'

'And what if I did go to the window? They'd no right to be keeping me prisoner.'

'They were doing the best they could for you,' Brunt tried to plead. 'It may not have been a very sparkling best, but if they hadn't tried, maybe you and I wouldn't be talking here this morning.'

Hypocrisy, he thought, but every instinct in him was for pushing her towards conciliation.

'They were trying to poison me,' she said.

She thought she knew that too, did she? What else did she think she knew?

'Mrs Hargreaves, Mrs Bagguley went out that morning. And her husband went out.'

'With his cart. With my furniture on it.'

'But you'd come to an arrangement with the Bagguleys about your furniture, hadn't you?'

'Arrangement!'

'You know that Mrs Bagguley came back early because the carrier's van had a broken axle? And you went to the window. And you saw someone come in.'

'I saw Geroge Ludlam come in.'

And she laughed—a sudden and hideous statement of her mind. Brunt saw what the key question had to be. He waited for her to stop laughing. When she did, she turned her head to look at him with an eye that was saying how much she could tell if she wanted to.

'Mrs Hargreaves, how did you know it was George Ludlam? How many years was it since you had seen him? If I'm not mistaken, not since the day of your accident. Fifty years ago—when you were both underfed children. Are you trying to tell me you recognized him? When had you last even thought about George Ludlam?'

'I don't want to talk to you.'

'Mrs Hargreaves, it's in your power to save a man's life.'

She said nothing.

'Mrs Hargreaves, you were at the window, and you saw George Ludlam come in. I'm not arguing with that. I know George Ludlam came in. And let's forget for the moment how you knew it was George Ludlam. Perhaps someone had told you that he was likely to come. But someone else came into Starve-Acre that morning, too—after Mrs Bagguley, and before George Ludlam.'

Eva Hargreaves's claw-like fingers at the end of her matchstick wrists began to scratch at her sheet, and when she had managed to grasp it, she snatched it roughly aside. Then she stuck out one leg, her bad leg, holding it out at a flagrantly macabre angle: her stock-in-trade, which she knew how to use, as an Indian beggar parades his sores.

'I'm going for a piss.'

'Mrs Hargreaves, you ought to be ashamed of yourself, so you should, talking like that with a gentleman present.'

Nurse Murphy was outraged.

'She's disgusting,' came a voice across the room.

Eva Hargreaves's nightdress was falling away from her emaciated frame, revealing shrunken breasts against the furrows of her ribs.

'Behave yourself decently now, Mrs Hargreaves.'

'He'll forget he's a gentleman if I show him much more,' Eva Hargreaves said, and began an unsteady walk down the centre of the ward, casting her crippled leg sideways in a manner that Brunt was sure was exaggerated.

'Can she manage on her own, then?' he asked.

'She can manage on her own if it suits her, and she'll fall over if she wants to make work for us. She'll remember anything she wants to remember, and if you press her any harder than you've been trying to press her, she'll stop knowing who she is and where she came from.'

'Why don't you take her away?' someone asked. 'When that policeman came to see her the other day, we thought he'd come to fetch her.'

'She's ruining this Infirmary.'

'She talks about George Ludlam in her sleep.'

'It's always George Ludlam.'

There were a handful of women in here, weak and withered, who had nevertheless retained their faculties. Brunt moved over among them.

'What sort of things does she say about him, then?'

'She hates him.'

'She's always on about him.'

'She hates him.'

'Yes—but why does she hate him?'

'She talks to him sometimes as if he was here.'

'She did last night.'

'What sort of things did she say?'

'Told him to mind his own business.'

'Told him he was forever stirring things up, making things worse for the others.'

'Said she wouldn't have had that broken leg if it wasn't for him.'

'How did she make that out, then?'

'She didn't say.'

It was hopeless. Brunt had to pretend to show interest while they told him things he already knew. He steered clear of leading questions: put an idea into their heads, and they would believe it was their own. He said a few more inconsequential things to them and then went back to Nurse Murphy.

'If she does say anything that you think might help us—in her sleep, or at any time—do you think you could note it down for me?'

Bridget Murphy looked hopelessly round at her forty charges.

'A fat lot of time I have for writing.'

'You know what I mean. If you could only *remember*. I'll be back sometime.'

'I'm not on nights, anyway. That's when you hear things.'

She rolled her eyes to the ceiling.

'She'll be back any minute. And you'll get no more from her. She'll do one of two things—I'm getting to know her— aren't we all, now? It'll either be a tantrum or her memory will have gone altogether. I'll settle for the tantrum if she sees you're still here. If you wouldn't mind, Mr Brunt—'

He did not have to mind. Thank God, Mrs Hargreaves wouldn't be admissible as evidence. Ludlam's lawyer would be asleep on his feet if he didn't scotch that. Otherwise she'd be the last plank in Ludlam's scaffold, even if she had to commit perjury.

Brunt put the railings of the Workhouse forecourt behind him. From a blue sky the sunshine was bathing Bakewell's bridge, church and river.

CHAPTER 15

On his return to Darley Dale, Brunt repaired immediately to the kitchen at The Alders. There was no culpable dereliction of duty in that. It was as sound a source of intelligence as he was likely to find in the village. And he still felt so unsure of Fanny Metcalfe that he did not appreciate how nervously glad she was to see him again after a gap of some twenty hours. But she had a working message for him: that his colleague Sergeant Nadin was upstairs in Matron's office, and that he was to report there as soon as he appeared.

Matron was not present. She had lent Nadin her room, in trepidation at the publicity that was already threatening her Home. Nadin was sitting at her desk, with Reginald Burdell and Amelia Carstairs seated well apart in front of him, both looking miserable. And the Sergeant—though the resemblance to an intelligent chimpanzee was still unavoidable—was looking brisker and more efficient than Brunt had ever seen or imagined him. He had taken copious statements, which he kept stacking and unstacking as he talked. His fingers looked as if they had to busy themselves somehow. It was a new image to Brunt—but then Brunt had never before seen him in the middle of a process that might go so badly wrong.

Burdell was talking, extremely ill at ease.

'Of course, I take all the points that you have made, Sergeant. And I further understand that you do not want to be seen to have fallen down on a case on which you have expended so much time, energy and talent. But perhaps if I were to have a word with your superior officer?'

Nadin disposed of that suggestion with a single short movement of one hand.

'I can tell you here and now that you would get no change whatever out of him.'

'But has so very much harm been done? The sum involved—five hundred pounds—is neither here nor there as far as I am concerned. Can we not call it a gift? I would in any case have wanted to give Miss Carstairs a fairly substantial going-away present.'

But Amelia Carstairs had now given up appealing. If it was an act that she was putting on, then her gifts were wasted outside the London theatre. Listening to her, parrying her falsity in Darley Dale churchyard, Brunt had at least had no doubts about her vivacity. When he had had to set her on getting a non-existent speck out of his eye, he had felt a sweet-breathed magnetism that he had had to combat. But now she was drained of all that, sapped, aged, and exhausted of all she normally lived for. She had been crying—and these had not been tears of deceit. They had run over her cheeks from the corners of her eyes, furrowing the paint. The grey in her hair was more apparent now. She must know that after a further spell in prison, she would not be in a strong position to take up her accustomed way of life again.

'If I have to go in the witness-box—' Burdell said.

'As you will,' Nadin put in.

'Then I shall make the strongest possible plea for lenience.'

'You'll be wasting your breath. She'll get five years this time. I'll spare her, and not tell you how old that will make her.'

Nadin smiled sweetly at Amelia.

'But I'll put in a word for you myself. I'll make sure you're put to work in the laundry.'

He turned to Brunt.

'Have you ever seen a woman's hair after a week in a steam laundry?'

Burdell leaned angrily forward.

'This is vindictiveness, Sergeant. I would never have believed that an Englishman—'

Nadin was wickedly unimpressed.

'I refuse to press charges. I will deny your evidence.'

Nadin tapped his sheaf of papers.

'You will find yourself embarrassed by what you have already signed. If I were you, I would see my solicitor. Ask him at what stage a man becomes guilty of misprision of felony.'

Amelia wound up a sob in a sigh.

'Actually—I *do* have a sick sister.'

'I know. And she has several names. We have met some of them in your records. You have collected enough funds on her behalf to endow a whole hospital.'

'And there is a doctor in Bonn who would help. I can show you correspondence I have had with him.'

'Anyone can write a letter, and most professional men will have the courtesy to reply. I fancy your letter from that doctor has been the rounds in many fashionable British watering-places. You ought to have gone to Le Touquet when you said you would.'

They were interrupted by the concerned appearance of Matron, pleading that not too much fatiguing pressure be put on an old man. When she saw how oppressed he looked, she became professionally stern and wanted to take him away—and, perhaps surprisingly, Nadin made no objection.

'My dear, we shall meet again,' he said to Amelia.

Amelia looked at him without much belief.

'In five years' time,' Nadin muttered.

All in all, Brunt was thinking, he would not have treated Burdell quite as Nadin had. But within the next quarter of an hour, Nadin's purpose became clear.

'Don't you feel sorry for him?' he asked Amelia.

'Why should I? It seems to me you've dolloped enough on my plate for me not to need other people's sorrows.'

'Have you ever felt sorry for any of your victims?'

'Why should I? They're not victims. I've robbed nobody, ever, Mr Nadin—I've given people pleasure. People have been ready to pay for it. They've weighed up the price and handed it over willingly.'

'That's a way of looking at it that the law doesn't share, Amelia—not when you're collecting for hard-luck cases that don't exist. And when the willing price was paid, you never had second thoughts about leaving them stranded.'

Amelia shrugged.

'Should I have lost sleep over that? They've all been men and women who had more than their share.'

'They may have had. But when you dropped them, you were always prepared to drop them pretty hard.'

'Who are you being sorry for now? The law doesn't say anything about sentiment, does it?'

'I'm interested, that's all. I'm interested in what goes on between you and these people—particularly old people. You do seem to have a way with them. When did you discover that? When did you start gravitating towards them?'

'I don't want to go on talking. It's none of your business. You've got your case—you've nailed the law on me. Can't you leave it at that? Do you think I care for any of the things that you're on about?'

'Yes, I do. I think you do care.'

'What are you trying to get from me now, Nadin?'

She looked at him with disgust. She had taken her arrest very hard indeed. The breakdown was not far off. Was that what Nadin was stabbing for?

'Mr Nadin—'

Yes—it was coming. All her pretences were pretty well exhausted.

'It won't be five years, will it?'

'It could well be. You're no newcomer. Just remind us what spells you've done already.'

'Six months, a year, eighteen months. I couldn't do five,

Mr Nadin. I couldn't *stand* five.'

'They'll reckon five's about the measure. What do you say, Tom?'

'They gave Sal Dawson five,' Brunt said, inventing ruthlessly.

'I'm just wondering if I can see a way out,' Nadin said.

'Oh no! Oh no you don't!'

Amelia, coarse realist, saw the wrong implications—and ruled them out.

'No, thank you very much. Which of you is it to be? One or both? Thank you, I'd rather do my five. I know how it works. I've talked to women it's happened to. You give all you've got—and you still find you've got five to do.'

'Steady now, steady. Let's not spoil an innocent friendship. It's just an idea that keeps hammering in my head. Were you ever a nurse, Amelia—I mean in the accepted sense of the word?'

'I never finished my training,' she said sulkily.

'No, I can imagine not. How long before they threw you out—a week?'

'Longer than that. What is all this?'

'It has to do with the way you and old people magnetize each other. Which was what I was trying to talk philosophically to you about just now. Only you kept biting my head off.'

'If you've got anything to say, say it,' she said. 'Otherwise get me taken away to that quiet little room.'

'I know an old lady who needs a lot of attention. She's not a nice old lady—but you might have to share that quiet little room with someone worse.'

'Stop talking riddles,' she said.

'It isn't a riddle. I'll come to the point, if you'll let me. You look after this old lady—in the proper sense. She also has information which we are finding it very difficult to get out of her.'

'Oh no—not Amelia. Amelia's always kept herself well

clear of that kind of dirt. I'd rather go to bed with the pair of you at once.'

'Don't be vulgar. What I am offering is that Tom and I would be quite ready to forget about Reggie Burdell—'

'You know very well you can't offer me any guarantee of that.'

'You'd be working for a solicitor—independently of us, if you insist. You need account only to him, if you don't trust us. You need not have any direct dealing with me and Tom. Need she, Tom?'

'Not if she doesn't want to,' Brunt said.

'I was talking to this solicitor yesterday, and I know there'd be a good deal more than just nursing pay in it for you, if you could pull it off. What they call an honorarium.'

'Where are you trying to take me? How do I know what to believe? And what are you two getting out of it?'

'I'll lay down my hand,' Nadin said. 'This solicitor has a practice in Derby. He's briefing defence counsel for a fellow called Ludlam—'

She looked up with the first sign of life she had shown.

'I've read about him in the papers. He's going to need that solicitor. He doesn't seem to have used the brains he was born with.'

'Well, maybe the papers have got their angles wrong. Tom and I happen to think, for a variety of reasons, that George Ludlam is in danger of becoming a classical miscarriage of justice. We would also like to see one of our inspectors doing some penance in public. Does that show you what's in it for Tom and me? And does it convince you?'

'It's beginning to sound daft enough to have something in it. How long is this going to tie me down?'

'How long, Tom?'

'A month at the outside,' Brunt said. 'It's got to be settled in a month. The trial—'

'And where's this old lady going to be nursed? Here?'

'Matron would love that, wouldn't she? No—Eva Hargreaves is at present keeping Bakewell Workhouse awake at nights. She is going to be transferred to an unpresumptuous little inn in a lonely corner of the hills, where you will stay with her. You will have your own room, live off the fat of the land—and also have for company a second old lady, one Annie Barker. I make it no secret that Annie will be keeping an eye on you.'

'I need time to think it over.'

'You can't have any. Tom and I are tired of Darley Dale. I'm being honest with you, Amelia, I think you may be in for a month's hell. It depends mostly on what Annie Barker thinks of you. But there are sixty months in a five-year stretch.'

'Can I talk to this solicitor?'

'Naturally.'

'Oh God, Amelia,' she said to herself. 'What are you letting yourself in for this time?'

'You ought to get into the habit of asking yourself that more often,' Nadin said. 'And now I suppose I'd better go and take a weight off Reggie's mind—before he goes belly-aching to Pickford.'

CHAPTER 16

Brunt saw nothing of Nadin for some days. One or two inquiries came his way, all of them petty, most of them involving him in laborious travelling, usually on foot, and all of them keeping him well away from Litton. He even had to go along the track of the Cromford and High Peak Railway between Ladmanlow and Diamond Hill: thefts from a train that had stood overnight when the engine had broken down. But he made his way eventually to Litton and decided to renew contact with village affairs in the Red Lion, Litton's other pub. The company there had no high society ideas about making oblique approaches.

'Is it business that brings you back up here, Mr Brunt?'

'Just had orders to keep a general eye on you lot,' he said, which did not go amiss with them.

'Rum set-up Annie Barker's got, over the road, then.'

Brunt knew he would have to tell them something, but he played for time, wanting to know how much they had put together for themselves.

'Well, if my name was Eva Hargreaves, I wouldn't mind ending up my days on Annie's cooking.'

'Who's that other woman she's got there? Some kind of nurse, is she?'

'Bloody good job old Isaac Slack's not still about,' someone said, 'with talent like that in the village.'

'Who's paying—that's what I'd like to know.'

'Well—it stands out a mile, doesn't it? He's paying.'

'You'd have thought he'd want every penny he could raise for his barrister.'

'Barrister? He'll need to be a bloody good barrister.'

'It only goes to show, doesn't it, you never can tell? He talked to me a time or two, and you'd think whatever he's been doing these years, it had turned him into a gent.'

'Aye, but quick-tempered. You could see he was quick-tempered. Blew his safety-valve when he saw the state Eva Hargreaves was in—and the knife was lying on the table—'

It was clear that Litton village had already condemned Ludlam. Brunt turned his head to see how Ben Bagguley was taking all this. Several others looked in the same direction. Bagguley was not far from drunk. He pushed the back of his hand across his mouth.

'Bastard!'

Brunt went down the road to Jack Judson's, found the constable cleaning his boots for tomorrow.

'Anything happening over at Annie's?' Judson asked.

'Don't know—haven't been over there yet. Just been collecting a few well-considered judgements in the Lion.'

Judson screwed a face.

'Not evidence, that.'

'But some pointers. Bagguley looks a mess.'

'Bagguley always was a mess.'

'How did they get on together, the Bagguleys? Were they a couple?'

'A couple means two. There were two of them.'

'You know what I mean, Jack.'

'I don't suppose they fought more than most of us do,' Judson said. 'Made a bit more noise about it, perhaps. But no—I mustn't give false impressions. I never knew strife at the Bagguleys that didn't stay within their own walls. She'd learned how not to provoke him when he'd had a drop too much. And when he got home nights, he was usually too far gone to do much more than fall asleep.'

'I ask, because he looks pretty lost.'

'I've known a man lost when a wife's died that he's gone hammer and tongs at all his life. You miss what you're used to. And Bagguley's not going to care for old folk on his own, is he?'

Bagguley was coming out of the Red Lion as Brunt went back up the street. Brunt stepped back into a doorway to watch him. The hill-scratching farmer had taken enough to affect his gait, but he knew where he was going. He lurched, caught a shoulder against a wall, righted himself, and then steered a course out of the village, making a false step every six or seven paces.

The word was that, thrown out by his married sister, he had gone back to Starve-Acre—a Starve-Acre starved of even Molly Bagguley's domestic attentions. Would he even have scrubbed out the mess where his wife had lain? Brunt's acquaintance with people and their habits had increased since he had first met Ludlam on a train.

CHAPTER 17

So to the Cordwainers'. There were a few in the bar now, the tavern having recovered its following since George Ludlam had gone from the scene. Annie Barker and Amelia were both behind the counter, Amelia looking as if she had functioned as a barmaid all her life, her hair piled up in an intricate structure that Brunt tried for many bemused minutes to trace to its basic system. Moreover, she had the fundamental ethos of the English barmaid, for she was a disciplinarian who would retain her popularity on all fronts. Like a regimental sergeant-major who hopes that the home depot will be his domain for the duration of a war, Amelia had taken the long view and established on her first parade the tone that was to last. Let a rude word overstep the well-defined range of what was permitted, let a crude habit threaten the poise of the house, and Amelia's eyebrow was arched and sighted on the offender.

Brunt had the immediate impression that Annie Barker had taken to Amelia without qualification. It might by no means necessarily have worked out so—but Annie seemed rotundly content to take a side-seat and let Amelia do the presiding. Brunt had his customary small beer, and Amelia gave him his change with practised fingers.

The company in the Cordwainers' was different from that in the Red Lion. Not more intelligent, not more refined, not less raucous—but with a different outlook, grouped round a different nucleus. There were some here who had known George Ludlam in the days that were now a very long way off: Peter Townley, Dick Logan, Harry Lockett.

'Yes, well—I'd like to see him talk his way out of it—he could always talk, could George.'

'It was talking that got him into half the trouble he was in down at Needham's—all that Justice of the Peace stuff.'

'Do you remember when Billy Orgill caught him and Dodger Green pinching treacle, and made them eat a seven-pound tin in front of the rest of us while he flicked them with the end of a coach-whip?'

'Dodger gave up.'

'George Ludlam didn't. He scraped down to the last spoonful. Remember how we cheered when he kicked the empty tin across the yard?

'Bloody rum sort of punishment, we thought at first, didn't we, having to eat bloody treacle? I know what I'd have have given to have got my bloody chops round a bloody spoon-ful—and Billy Orgill wasn't hitting them all that bloody hard—just keeping them bloody awake, you might say.'

'You have just used that word six times,' Amelia said.

'What word was that, then, ma'am?'

Peter Townley's offended innocence sounded genuine.

'I'm not going to sully my lips with it,' she said. 'I'm just going to ask you if you know what it means, that's all.'

'Well, it means covered with blood, doesn't it, same as you and I have in our veins?'

'It does not, Mr Townley. Besides, there was no blood in the treacle-tin—and none round your chops.'

She said the last word as if it were something nauseating that she was trying to get off the tip of her tongue.

'I will tell you what it means. It is what the dictionary people call a corruption. It stands for *By Our Lady* and you never know who is listening when you talk, Mr Townley, or whose susceptibilities might be offended.'

There were several words in this speech that Peter Town-ley could not have defined, but he saw their sum total.

'Sorry, ma'am.'

And thereupon Annie Barker began a routine for which she was famous. In those days of unrestricted licensing hours, the times of shutting doors depended on the outlook of the landlord, and this was a subject on which Annie Barker was inflexible. She liked her night's rest and had long since ceased to rely on verbal hints. Her broom was the scourge of her public bar, and it suddenly came up in her hand now with the violence that had been known to send strangers scooting into the street. Her fat globular figure appeared to be rolling behind it and in effect she did little more to the accumulated dust than to raise it in all directions. She swept under chairs that men were sitting on, swept the toes of their boots, and if there were anyone present so unfamiliar with the campaign as to raise his bottom half an inch from his seat, that seat was gone from under him and the broom-handle was throwing him off-balance from behind his knees.

'You've two minutes to finish your pots, or it all goes back into the ullage.'

'Now, steady on, Annie. That was my bad ankle.'

'There's only one thing wrong with your ankle, same as is wrong with the rest of you. It's steeped in bitter beer.'

Within two minutes, as always, they were out in the street—and Brunt, waiting for private talk was leaning his head against the bar counter, laughing like a school-boy.

But not for long. The broom came clattering between his feet.

'What's the matter with you, then, Tom Brunt? Haven't you a home to go to?'

'It isn't that,' Brunt said. 'I wanted a word.'

'He wants a word,' Annie said to Amelia. Her broom had now come up to the position known to the military as porte arms, and its bristles, with a tangle of thread hanging from them, were shaking an inch from Brunt's nose.

'Well, go on—say your word!'

'I just wanted to find out how things are going.'

'He wants to find out how things are going,' Annie repeated, as if Amelia were incapable of picking up anything for herself.

'What things was it you were wondering about, Mr

Brunt?' Amelia asked him. 'We're all doing fine. I found it hard work, putting fresh barrels on, at first. But I'm beginning to get the feel of it.'

'You know very well what I mean.'

'We will if you tell us.'

'Will you just stand aside, so I can get into that corner?' Annie asked him. Brunt obeyed with the alacrity of a man who believed that her next move might be a crack across his shins.

But then there came three thumps on the floor upstairs, as from an invalid whose equipment included a stout old walking-stick.

'She'll be wanting her nightcap,' Annie said.

'I'll see to it.'

Amelia went into the kitchen and came back with a heavy black kettle. She began mixing a hot port and lemon.

'That'll be Eva Hargreaves?' Brunt asked.

'Well, I should hope so. I've only got one up there. This isn't the Manchester Infirmary.'

Amelia came out from behind, carrying the drink cautiously on a tray. Brunt opened the stair-bottom door for her, giving himself the sly opportunity to leave it open.

'How is she, then, the old girl?'

'There's not much wrong with Eva Hargreaves. She'll see some of us under the daisies.'

'Picked up, has she? I'm glad to hear it. Has she—?'

'Has she what?'

'Has she said anything?'

'Plenty.'

'I dare say,' he said. 'But has she said enough?'

'Has that anything to do with you?' Annie asked him.

'I should have thought so. Now come on, Annie—'

'We were given to understand that you'd handed it all over: that it's all between Amelia and a Derby solicitor. She's a good lass, is Amelia. I wish she were staying here for good. Do you think you and Jimmy could persuade her?'

From upstairs there came a woman's laughter—in which they heard Amelia join. There was more than a hint of unkindness in the first woman's cackle—but it was spontaneous, and it was Eva Hargreaves. There were natives of Litton who would claim that they had never heard her laugh.

'See what I mean,' Annie Barker said. 'She has a way with people.'

'Let's hope she can go the whole way. There isn't much time. The trial—'

'Oh, she's been down to Derby and seen the solicitor.'

'That's what I'm getting at, Annie. We need to know—'

Annie shook her head.

'That's not what he told her. He says it's better for you not to know.'

'Look, Annie—there's a man tossing and turning in Derby Gaol, knowing that before long they'll be testing the drop with a sandbag.'

'Aye—and if it's left to the efforts of some people, he'll be following that sandbag. Leave it alone, Tom Brunt. You and Jimmy Nadin put your heads together, and just for once you had a good idea—you had the sense to leave it to three women.'

Brunt looked at her helplessly. There were some battles that could not be fought with Annie Barker. Amelia came back down the stairs, still smiling to herself.

'Can she have a hunk of bread and cheese, Annie?'

'What—at bedtime?'

'I think she's had all the nightmares there are—wide awake.'

'Give her anything she wants,' Annie said.

Amelia went into the kitchen.

'See what happens to a woman when somebody shows that they like her,' Annie said. 'That's another one up to Amelia. She says if people see that you like them, you can do anything you want with them.'

'She ought to know. I wish somebody liked me,' Brunt said.

'There are times when we show that best by telling you nothing.'

'I don't see that.'

'You wouldn't.'

Amelia came back carrying a sandwich that looked like the foundation stone for a Nonconformist chapel.

'Is Thomas Brunt trying to understand what loving people means?' she asked. 'So who is Thomas Brunt's neighbour? Listen, Detective—no man who knows what love means could be a policeman.'

They were united against him. They were enjoying themselves, determined to keep their achievements—if any—to themselves. And Brunt was worried. This had got out of hand—out of his hands and Nadin's. If it went wrong, it was going to be the end of the earth's foundations when it fetched up on Pickford's desk. And by that time, it would be a little late to do anything constructive for Ludlam.

Brunt needed Nadin. He needed him despite the hour. It was after eleven before he left the Cordwainers', well aware that the eldritch laughter was still going on as he walked down the street. It took him an hour and a half—mercifully all downhill—to reach Miller's Dale station. There, thanks to the variety of his acquaintances, he got a lift into Buxton goods yard on the footplate of a coal train. The magic lights of shunting signals, the evocative smell of heavy oil, the choking solidity of the fumes in the tunnels: there was a nostalgia here for the boy Brunt who had once wanted to drive an engine; and also a deadening conviction that it was a little late in the day to be contemplating the change.

It was well after two o'clock when he got to Nadin's bachelor lodging. But calls in the middle of the night were something with which Nadin and his landlady always had to reckon. And Nadin was always quick to wake, as alert in two seconds as if he had not been asleep. At the sight of the obviously disturbed Brunt, he was surprisingly sweet-tempered. But Brunt's first few sentences were too heartfelt to be clear.

'I tell you—they've got the answer—or think they have—and they're keeping it to themselves.'

'You might as well keep it to *your*self, if this is the best way you can tell me.'

Nadin was sitting on the edge of the bed in his nightshirt and had partly inserted his feet into carpet slippers.

'Start at the beginning, lad.'

'They seem to know—Eva Hargreaves must have told them—'

'They know, do they?'

'They know a lot. And they wouldn't tell me. And Amelia Whatever-you-care-to-call-her has been to see Ludlam's solicitor.'

'That's fine,' Nadin said.

'Yes—but we need to know too, don't we?'

'No,' Nadin said. 'Where are your brains, Tom? We're better off not knowing, at this stage.'

'I wouldn't have thought that that was ever true at any stage.'

'Tom—why are we doing this?'

'To get George Ludlam off.'

'At Pickford's expense, Tom—I've got rather less time left in this Force than Ludlam has before he sees the inside of the topping-shed.'

'Therefore—'

'Therefore my time for smiting Pickford is equally thin. And I'm going to do that, Tom. If I've achieved nothing else since I first planted the soles of my feet along Friar Street, I'm going to bring Pickford down.'

He had said the same thing before, but somehow it had never carried the bitterness that it did now. Perhaps that was because he was so near to it, but not quite there yet.

'I'm going to bring Pickford down, and if I come unstuck, I

shall have nothing to cry about. But if I come unstuck, I don't want you unstuck with me.'

'That's very nice of you—but it's all the more reason for needing to know what's happening.'

'All the more reason why we're better off ignorant. Listen: Pickford's a pig—and several other things that it's healthier for me not to let my mind dwell on. But just remember: he isn't being dishonest about George Ludlam. He believes Ludlam's guilty—and he's been a policeman long enough to know that evidence alone is not enough. Damn it, haven't we all found that to our cost before now? He doesn't want to fake evidence against Ludlam—he just wants to make sure nothing's out of balance, nothing unaccounted for that will play into the hands of the defence. He doesn't want what he sees as red herrings dangled in front of the jury.'

Nadin scratched his ribs.

'So Eva Hargreaves knows more than she's let on. So Amelia has worked it out of her. So Amelia travels to Derby, sees Ludlam's solicitor. So Ludlam's solicitor realizes that this is the beginning of a let-out for Ludlam. But only the beginning, that's my guess. They won't be wanting to put Eva Hargreaves up for cross-examination, will they? There's no mystery about who killed Molly Bagguley. Eva knows—as you and I do, don't we, Tom? But the defence are probably still a long way from proving it. Until they can do that, they're not going to hand it back to you and me, so that we can feed it back to Pickford—so that he can get his counter-punches ready. Not on your life. That's why those women have been told to keep their mouths shut.'

'You said just now—'

'Pickford's going to be knocked cold, and you and I aren't even going to have to hit him, Tom. That appeals to me—though I hope I shall be in court to see the blow fall. All you and I have to do is carry on looking for fishing-rods, and coal pilfered off railway tenders—and let Pilkington, Hargreaves, Barker and Co. work for the law.'

Nadin made it sound feasible. For a short minute, Brunt believed it might come true. But Nadin's confidence did not really convince him. Brunt did not care for letting go of the strings.

CHAPTER 18

The Ludlam trial opened, and there was no hint to the outside world that the defence intended catapulting a whiff of slingshot across the courtroom. The opening speeches were plain. The prosecution was relying heavily on timings, would show that the murdered woman had intended being away from Litton for the morning, but had returned unexpectedly. Her husband had also been away, selling a cartload of second-hand furniture in Eyam. The accused would not—could not—deny that he had taken advantage of the absence of the pair to pay a visit to an old friend of his, whom they were nursing. He knew he was unwelcome in that house. He had been denied access on one occasion and had effected an illegal entry on another. He had been found (by Tommy Lamp-oil) actually handling the corpse, and his body and clothes bore bloodstains.

It was unspectacular: and the court reporters had to make do with such human elements as they saw before them. They described George Ludlam as quiet and unharassed, and appearing to take a keen interest in the proceedings.

The Crown would go on to show that there had been a personal relationship in an unhappy past between the prisoner and the elderly woman whom the Bagguleys were caring for. He had made general inquiries in the village about her welfare and had been disturbed by irresponsible rumours that he had heard.

Mr Hartwell, for the defence, claimed that there was an unaccounted time-lapse between the killing of Mrs Bagguley and the prisoner's entry into the farmhouse. It was very convenient for the prosecution to gloss over this gap as if it did not exist. Unfortunately for the neatness of their case, there had been such a gap. And although the loss of blood and the relative shortness of the interval made it impossible for experts to speak usefully of the time of death, a scientific witness would be sworn to show that the nature of the fouling of the prisoner's clothing could not have come from arterial bleeding in full flow.

Equally inconclusive was the question of George Ludlam's left-handed or right-handedness. Medical evidence showed that Mrs Bagguley had had her throat cut from behind by a right-handed man. George Ludlam was left-handed—though an attempt had been made to prove him ambidextrous—a ludicrously clumsy and unscientific experiment which the investigating officer would later be asked to describe for himself.

The witnesses on the first afternoon were mainly concerned with discovery and arrest. Tommy Lamp-oil, looking for once as if he wished he had no information to impart, was eased through a factual account of coming upon George Ludlam trying to lift the body of Molly Bagguley.

PC Judson gave evidence of having been called and proceeding to Starve-Acre. No, sir: the prisoner had made no effort to avoid arrest. Judson had found him sitting disconsolate on a stone outside the farm, and he had accompanied him without fuss to the police-house.

Inspector Pickford gave his testimony with efficiently restrained pomp. He had a parade-ground voice, which he knew how to discipline. He created the impression of a patient, experienced and detached man,

'Will you tell the court what view you have formed about the left-handedness or otherwise of the prisoner.'

'I have formed no opinion on that point.'

'Nevertheless, you performed an experiment for which you considered it worth transporting my client back to Litton.'

'A shot in the dark, sir. Inconclusive. I have to concede that the effort was not worth the while.'

'You mean it did not produce the desired result?'

'I mean the result produced was neither here nor there.'

Ben Bagguley was called next, a man who had wiped if not scrubbed himself for the occasion and had put on newer (though not new) clothes than any in which men had ever seen him before. Nicks over his cheeks and chin bore witness to the thoroughness with which he had shaved. And he was sober.

He was treated with exemplary courtesy by both sides. Mr Broome indeed opened with an apology for calling him at all, so sad a man, now being compelled to suppress understandable emotions under the public gaze. Mr Bagguley looked distrustful of this. He never did fully trust well-spoken men.

He was Benjamin Bagguley, farmer and general dealer, and on the day in question he had left his home at eight in the morning to carry a cartload of furniture to Mr Wilfred Hearnshaw's establishment at Eyam. He had not left Eyam on his homeward journey until after midday, and he had been met with grievous news late in the afternoon, when by chance he had encountered an itinerant oil-chandler.

Mr Hartwell was soft-tongued and also apologetic. He asked only one question, and that was to draw the admission that the load of furniture in question had been the former property of Mrs Eva Hargreaves.

His Lordship appeared to be making a vain search among his papers.

'This is not the first time, Mr Hartwell, that we have heard reference to this woman. And yet I do not appear to have read any deposition by her.'

'Mrs Hargreaves, m'lud, is elderly and in some mental confusion. She is not believed to be in a condition to help the court.'

And Mr Broome, prosecuting, was also on his feet.

'That is common ground between us, m'lud.'

The judge looked unhappy. But then, he was known to be an unhappy judge.

'Yet she seems to have been in a fit state of mind to have disposed of her household effects.'

Adjournment. And Mr Hartwell and George Ludlam's solicitor kept their inner feelings to themselves. The public gallery saw two lawyers quietly satisfied at the end of an uneventful day. But the event for which they had been waiting all day had not happened. They were awaiting word from Litton that three women had succeeded in a certain course of action. And in case the three women failed, the same course of action had been entrusted to a private investigator. No encouraging message had come in from either party.

They went and saw Ludlam under the court before he was taken away for the night. This was partly to nourish his morale, but also to tell him that he must be prepared to go into the witness-box, and that the longer his examination could be drawn out, the better. A decision about this had been delayed for reasons that are common in such cases. George Ludlam himself was enthusiastic about putting in a personal appearance. He was a truthful man with nothing to hide, confident of his ability to convince twelve fellow citizens of his plain-speaking, reliable maturity. Mr Hartwell was not so sanguine. Plain-speaking about Needham's mill, Eva Hargreaves and Ben Bagguley might involuntarily implant in the minds of the jury a clear motivation to murder.

But now Hartwell saw no choice. They might have to try to keep Ludlam in the box all day. They might need the time. In theory, he could be saved at any time before the hangman pulled his lever. Procedurally, it was tidier and safer to get him acquitted now—and to achieve that, any fresh evidence had to be put in before the closing speeches.

The solicitor made a late afternoon call on the Chief Constable. He did not think that preliminaries with Inspector Pickford would get him far.

CHAPTER 19

When the calls for action came, they came urgently. Pickford, for example, had been sent for from home by the Chief
Constable. The evening press had not, in fact, given the
Inspector a bad paragraph; but the Chief Constable, after
listening to Ludlam's solicitor, had been taking a close look
at the casenotes.

'Easy case, Pickford, obvious culprit—so simplify the
evidence and obliterate all crosstrails. In nine cases out of ten
it works,' the Chief Constable said. 'No injustice is done, and
no harm. This time I can see both on the horizon.'

'Sir?'

'Three women have been stirring up the bottom of the
pool. They've produced some very dubious evidence but it
could be developed. You have to look at it from every angle
including angles that might look the opposite of helpful. You
ought not to need me to tell you that.'

'No, sir.'

'I hope you're not going to be proved wrong, Pickford. But
if you are, let the admission come from you. Don't wait to be
accused. You might be able to shelter behind the fact of fresh
evidence. But Pickford—'

Pickford never forgot that he had been an army captain,
but he looked just now like a reprimanded corporal.

'Pickford, I am not myself a man given to seeking shelter. I
prefer to stand up straight in the open spaces. Get to Litton
tonight. I have it on good authority that there are inns in the
place.'

So there was a convergence on Litton. Amelia had rushed to
Buxton in a hired carriage. Nadin had had to be fetched from
the theatre. Brunt was met at the railway station gates: he

had been using his phenomenal knowledge of train-times to make a personal evening visit to Darley Dale.

'We are stuck,' Amelia said, in a bleak office corner in the police station in Higher Buxton. 'And it's my fault. I thought I could do it on my own.'

She was nervous—something new in Brunt's and even Nadin's knowledge of her. When defeated in the past she had—except when prison itself seemed unavoidable—had the ultimate comfort of a philosophy that took troubles as they came. But her role in the Cordwainers' Arms had been different. She had got caught up in what she was doing. She had left too late the admission that she could not finish what she had started.

'It wasn't true that I'd been to see the solicitor. I went the next day. He was interested—keenly interested—but not satisfied. There were other questions that he wanted answered. I was sure that Annie and I between us could get those answers. It's sickening. We're there—and yet we're not there. We can't use the word of a woman who the world thinks is crazed. They won't put her in the box. I wish they'd let me question her in the box. And I wish I'd come back to you earlier. I went to Eyam—but all I got was a stronger case for the prosecution.'

There were no recriminations. Brunt left the talking to Nadin. And just as it was a new Amelia, so it was a new Nadin: patient, kindly, communicating no sense of doubt, putting on the façade of a leisurely, undisturbed man.

'Well, let's get the major mystery out of the way first,' he said.

'Major mystery?' She laughed emptily. 'No mystery at all, of course.'

'Ben Bagguley?'

'It had to be, hadn't it? Eva saw him come and go again—before Ludlam came. A plain case of wife-murder. But the man Hearnshaw in Eyam can't be shifted. Bagguley did not leave until after twelve noon. So how could he have been in Eyam and Litton at the same hour? How did he dispose of that horse and his cartload of furniture? And how is it that no one in Litton caught sight of him?'

'Suffice it to say,' Nadin said, 'that these things took place. There's a formula that I've always fallen back on, whenever I've been faced with the impossible: it happened. He did it by doing it.'

'But we've still got to prove it. The solicitor asked me those questions. I was sure that anything Bagguley could do, I could find out about. Annie could get people putting their ears to the ground. But there's no information to be got. How do you set about cases like this, Jimmy?'

'You ought to have joined us years ago, Amelia. Then you'd have learned. But we shall achieve nothing here. We need to be in Litton. Tomorrow needs an early start. We have a lot to get done while the lawyers keep the talk going.'

Within no time they were rattling beside the moonlit Wye in a jobber's carriage.

'I didn't think I was going to make any progress with Eva at first,' Amelia said. 'I'd rather take on a retired General, any day of the week. Her stock in trade is lack of reason—it has been all her life—a rhinoceros hide of unreason. And it's a weapon to reckon with. Pancras Workhouse, Needham's mill, Litton village. She's known all along that George Ludlam didn't kill Molly. She says she doesn't know whether she'd have let him hang for it or not—but she was certainly going to make him wait. And do you know why? Because whatever he may say about it, it was George Ludlam's fault that her leg got broken. Against her wishes, he'd given her name as a witness to some Needham atrocity. That's why she was put under the machine. But let me go back a bit.

'She had bronchitis in the early winter weeks of this year. She was very ill indeed and doesn't remember much about it: fever, bad dreams, Tommy Lamp-oil calling, Molly Bagguley bringing her broth. Tots of brandy, a witch's brew of homemade cough-mixture, thick with honey and vinegar, a steam-kettle, coal-tar vapour. She recognized that it had to be the Bagguleys, the Workhouse or death. She was in no state to think things out. To save journeys, the Bagguleys moved her up to Starve-Acre. There was talk about what was to be done with her furniture. She still can't remember agreeing to anything. There were days when she'd have agreed to anything to silence Molly Bagguley's voice.

'She began to get better. Maybe some of the folk-remedies had their effect. She also had an inner core: stamina. There came a morning when she knew where she was and what she was doing there—and what was likely to happen next. She believed all the stories she had heard about the Bagguleys. She knew that she was relatively safe for a week or two. With both Nell Merridew and Isaac Slack, there had had to be a period when the nursing looked genuine—and they would have to be specially careful a third time. She decided to feign senile stupidity, not to understand what it did not suit her to understand. Her strength would gradually return, and one day, she did not know how, but she would watch her opportunities, she would make good her escape. Where to? She did not care. Something would come her way. She had been surviving ever since she had been a bare-arsed kid on stone steps.

'She knew about the opiates. She knew about the taste of Crescent Mixture. As often as not she'd kept a bottle at home against chills and rheumatics. She'd spit a mouthful out when Molly Bagguley left the room—into the chamberpot, the fireplace. She knew how to act as if the stuff was having a potent effect, would pretend to be in a drugged sleep when she wanted to be left alone—and so that she could overhear things.

'And she did overhear things. The partition wall between hers and the Bagguleys' bedroom was thin. They were careless. She heard all the rumours when Ludlam came back to the village.

'She had always hated George Ludlam. It was so old a

hatred that she could hardly remember how it had begun. She says she remembers him when he was a tiny infant in the Pancras. Then she had been moved to Nottingham a year or more ahead of him. She had forgotten his existence—but all the ancient hatred returned. She snubbed him whenever she could.

'And he was a troublemaker right from the start. He was always trying to talk people into fighting for their rights—people who knew only too well that they hadn't any rights. He probably had more thrashings than any other boy in the mill—yet he never seemed to learn. Well, if he wanted seven floggings a week, that was his choice: but all the time, he was making things worse for the others. They were always tightening the discipline because of agitators like George Ludlam. He said he had written a letter to the Pancras Overseers because of a vicious attack on a seven-year-old. Eva had seen the incident, and he had let it be known that he had put her name in the letter as a witness. He must have talked indiscreetly to someone about it, for somehow, it got to John Needham's ears. That was why she was put under the machine: as a warning to her—

'And now George Ludlam was in the village, an aging but well-to-do man, so it seemed, and Ben Bagguley was telling his wife how the village was worried: because there were some like Billy Orgill who thought he was here to settle fifty-year-old scores. Then, be damned, he was knocking on the door of Starve-Acre, wanting to come in and see her. She heard him turned away, saw him the next time he came—the day he broke in. She stood by the window to watch, could barely keep from laughing when Molly Bagguley chased him off with that useless gun.

'I didn't think I was going to get anywhere with her at first,' Amelia repeated. 'And it didn't look as if Annie Barker was going to make any progress either. We heaped kind-nesses on her—food that we found she liked, tots when she fancied them. She seemed to resent kindness. It was talking to her about London that broke the ice. It so happens that I'm not exactly a stranger to the parts she was dragged up in: King's Cross, the Cally Market, Kentish Town. I talked to her about how different things are now—some things— and I suddenly realized that she had started asking me questions. After that—well, there was still uphill work to be done.'

They had come to the bottom of Ashwood Dale now and had started the long climb up Topley Pike. The horse's hooves became slower, until the male passengers had to be asked to get out and walk behind. Conversation could not start again until they reached the Miller's Dale turning.

'I don't know how long she'd have kept her mouth shut about who killed Molly Bagguley. By the way—I don't know what sort of a fellow this Ludlam is. I've heard descriptions and of course I've read the papers and Annie Barker seems besotted by him.'

And so Amelia had penetrated to the truth. Ben Bagguley had come home one night overcharged with excitement and beer—and the news that George Ludlam was rooting about in the Nell Merridew and Isaac Slack histories. There followed a mighty quarrel between the Bagguleys. Eva Hargreaves did not catch all that was said. Ben Bagguley's voice was slurred, and they were talking about things that they did not need to explain to each other. But it was all about who was to blame for the things that had been done.

This made Molly Bagguley very angry indeed. She was going to have nothing to do with harming Eva. She had had nothing to do with harming the other two. All she had ever done was to work herself silly as an unpaid nurse. But Bagguley was a man who never wanted to have to wait for anything. All they had needed to do with Nell Merridew and Isaac Slack had been to wait. If he went on with this stupid talk of hurrying Eva Hargreaves on her way, then she would be down at Jack Judson's first thing in the morning, would tell him the truth and clear herself.

'You're in it as deeply as I am,' Bagguley had said. 'You gave them the medicine.'

But Molly Bagguley seemed to be driven out of her mind by her fears of what George Ludlam was up to. In the morning, Bagguley might have forgotten—but his wife reminded him. It was either hands off Eva Hargreaves, or she went to the police. Bagguley chuntered and went across the yard to load furniture from a shed. It was Eva's own furniture: her bed, her husband's chair, her rocker, her old kitchen table. Her heart was sick to see it all go, to remember that now she had nowhere to take it to—and to know that there would be no way of getting any of it back.

Molly Bagguley was going shopping in Chapel-en-le-Frith. Eva suspected that that was with the small horde of sovereigns that she had kept in a tin under a floorboard: ten of them. But within an hour Molly Bagguley was back, and so, very shortly afterwards, was her husband. Eva watched him come stealthily from corner to corner of his outbuildings. He must have attacked his wife as soon as he was in the house. There was a scream reminiscent of a pig-killing, some stumbling about—and then silence. Bagguley stamped out. About twenty minutes later, Eva, sitting up in bed, saw George Ludlam approach. She sank down and prepared to feign coma.

'And she really would have let George Ludlam face the music?' Brunt asked.

'As one woman of another, I'd like to think she'd have relented after she thought he'd suffered suspense enough,' Amelia said. 'But in fact I don't think she cared. George Ludlam was interfering again. He was going to pay for it this time. She's not a *nice* woman, Mr Brunt.'

They drove through the village of Miller's Dale, the moon catching ripples where trout were breaking the water.

'You've done well,' Nadin said.

'Up to a point. We're still stuck.'

'There are one or two things that still need looking at.'

'We've no time.'

'We've tonight and most of tomorrow.'

The hill up to Tideswell: again Brunt and Nadin had to walk.

'It's going to need tight handling,' Brunt said.

'We've got things to go at. I've broken cases open on less—and in less time. It means we've got to lean on Amelia.'

'She'll be glad to get back to a life of honest crime.'

'She's learning all the time,' Nadin said. 'Now we've got to do something that Pickford tried to do. Only Amelia's got to make it work.'

Brunt did not make the necessary connection.

'She's got to get a confession from Bagguley. We can't rely on anything less to get Ludlam off.'

'Dangerous,' Brunt said.

'Aye, dangerous. If it were anyone less than Amelia, I wouldn't let her do it.'

'I'm not quite with you,' Brunt said.

'Of course you aren't.' Nadin unexpectedly clapped him on the shoulder. 'Because I've not told you all I've got on my mind. There isn't time, for one thing. For another—'

The carriage-lights were playing on Nadin's features with a sickly flickering yellow, accentuating shadows, emphasizing his age and end-of-career weariness. But even apart from the accidents of the light, there were differences about Nadin. The monkey-like features had about them a new dedication.

'I've sometimes dreamed of this happening, Tom. I've never had the nerve to believe that it actually would. I'd just made Sergeant when Pickford came back from the Crimea—without a day's police-work to his name. I've had him on my back ever since. Next Tuesday, my time's up. But Pickford's time is going to be up by this time tomorrow.'

The road levelled to a milder gradient for a stretch and they were all able to ride again. Nadin, peering out to where the lamps were faintly illuminating the roadside banks, suddenly called to the cabby to stop—which the horse, oddly, did not seem to want to do.

Nadin was out and ten yards back along the road, Brunt behind him, not knowing what he had spotted: a sturdy but huddled body fallen against tree-roots. Nadin struck a wax vesta and cupped his hand round it: Ben Bagguley, breathing noisily, not far from the threshold of alcoholic poisoning. He was on his way home from giving his evidence. No one would perhaps ever know in what unfamiliar tavern he had got himself into this state. The relatively respectable clothes that he had donned for the witness-box were now in a condition to take their place alongside the rest of his wardrobe.

'Give us a hand with him, Tom.'

Brunt thought that Nadin intended to take him in now—but it was only a question of dragging him behind a clump of brambles out of sight of the road.

'Because we don't want any Good Samaritan returning him to Starve-Acre before we've finished up there, do we?'

Bagguley started pawing at them as they lifted him—but there was neither strength nor coordination in his body. No sooner had he called for effort from his muscles than his limbs flopped uselessly at his sides, the backs of his huge hands scarred and horny. At the same time he was trying to say something. It was a pathetic effort to pronounce his wife's name—*Molly*—but it bubbled to nothing on his chapped lips, like the cry of a sick child whose fever has sapped it of the strength to call for its mother. Not with tenderness, but without violence, Nadin lowered his shoulders to the ground.

'A bad man, Tom—as bad as they come. I know what the judge will say to him, but I don't know what his Creator will—unless to apologize for not having made a better job of him.'

Nadin did not make to go straight back to the carriage. Instead, he stood back, as if to look at the prone heap that was Bagguley—though in effect nothing could be seen of him but a thickening of the shadows.

'You must think I have a funny attitude, Tom, for one who's spent a lifetime with men like Bagguley. I wonder what you'll be thinking of men like that, thirty years from now. Bad men? A man can't be what he hasn't been given the mechanics to be. Oh, as far as Ben Bagguley's concerned, you might as well hang him as try to do anything else with him, I suppose.'

Out on the road, the horse was becoming restive, trying to pull the carriage into the bank. The cabby was cursing him.

'Ben and Molly Bagguley, Tom: a life of hatred for each other. A life of mutual suspicion and mutual deception. Yet they stayed together, because neither of them had the guts to try anything new. And they made each other do things. They knew each other's way of scheming. Each knew the weaknesses that would destroy the other. He did away with her in panic: and now he can't bear to be without her. He misses even her hostility, because that was part of him. But I've said it before, Tom—you never know for certain which way a stunted intelligence will go.'

They climbed back into the carriage and Nadin addressed himself to Amelia.

'I don't claim to know what goes on in high places—and we're forty miles from Derby. But I can guess that someone, maybe the Chief himself, will have had an impressive word with Pickford by now: because the word I've had is that the solicitor's been to headquarters. So Pickford should be on his way to Litton too—and let's hope he's behind us, not in front.'

'He will be,' said Brunt, who knew his trains. 'He can't make Miller's Dale before—'

'Good. So he'll make for the Cordwainers' at whatever hour and never mind who has to be got out of bed. He mustn't see you on any account, Amelia. I don't know what he'd do—but he'd never make head or tail of what you were doing there. Annie will know how to keep you out of his way. But as soon as you get indoors, you've got to use every influence you can over Eva Hargreaves. She's got to regress, Amelia. She's got to have a relapse—she's got to go back to the state she was in. She's got to know nothing. She mustn't talk half a dozen words of consecutive sense in Pickford's presence.'

Amelia was nodding keenly.

'Because Pickford will be under orders to get hold of any new evidence there is, and he will at least have set out with that intention. But if he sees the slightest chance of going back to the Chief with his original theory proved, he's going to be sorely tempted.'

'That won't be difficult,' Amelia said. 'Eva will prefer it that way. I'd go so far as to call it Eva's way.'

'Your difficulty will come tomorrow morning, when Tom and I come for you.'

'You're still making me work for my liberty, aren't you?'

'Not only yours,' Nadin said. 'And try to hold on to it afterwards.'

CHAPTER 20

Nadin and Brunt alighted before they reached the lower end of Litton. They picked their way like hunting cats from one shadow to the next. Not that there was a soul out of doors— but the carriage-wheels were bound to bring some eyes to curtain edges.

They made their way to Starve-Acre, skirted the messy yard so as to make their approach from behind the farm-house. The key was under the slate under the water-butt.

'Hunt about for a few bits of candle, Tom. The Bagguleys must have made some efforts to light the place.'

Brunt found and lit a stub. Nadin stood in the middle of the room and surveyed it.

'Yes, well—we know where he did it. He came up from that corner, seizing the knife from the table. A right-handed slash, a powerful man's weight behind it. Now the sort of wound that goes through to the spine produces a lot of blood in a short time. Most of it's gushing away from Bagguley— but he gets in a mess, all the same. Ludlam got in a mess, even after the gushing had stopped. So Bagguley had to have a change of clothing within the next few minutes.'

'I don't suppose he could fall back on all that many changes of raiment.'

'He deals in anything—old clothes, for instance—and by that I mean stuff that he could only trade as rags. And Bagguley's no sartorial purist. We shall find a pile of old stuff awaiting transit in one of his sheds: the sort of heap where he could go in a bad moment for shirt, jacket and trousers. And I think we shall find the remnants of a fire somewhere. One day science will come to our aid and we'll be able to boil ashes in a test-tube and find out if there was blood on what was burned. Till then, we'll have to be satisfied with pointers.'

'We shall need more than pointers to find out how he managed to go to Eyam and not go to Eyam,' Brunt said.

'Patience, Tom, patience. Obviously he had an interrupted journey to Eyam. Come the dawn, we shall see the light.'

'I wonder how much sleep George Ludlam's getting these nights.'

'I'm only sorry for Ludlam up to a point. Eva Hargreaves may not be entirely wrong about him. Anyway—chilly though the thought may be, I'd rather find me a bundle of Ben Bagguley's hay out of doors than breathe in much more of the air of this happy household.'

And once out of doors, Nadin was miraculously asleep in

no time, but Brunt found it impossible to keep his eyes shut. The Bagguleys' yard was not a quiet place. More than once about his work, Brunt had kept vigil in places where the creaking of floorboards, the settlement of hinges, the sighing of draughts had seemed to impart a sort of soul to the environment. But it was a troubled soul that was created by the surroundings of Starve-Acre. A broken door swung and clapped. A hanging gutter scraped against a wall. The effect was restlessness, a reflection of the fecklessness of this couple. Brunt expected someone to arrive at any moment demanding to know what they were doing there. It would be Pickford, of course. If Pickford got as far as the Cordwainers', he was sure to come for a second look at Starve-Acre.

The first grey of dawn took a long time to declare itself and, after the promise of the first streaks, was agonizingly slow to develop. At last a certain rosiness was undeniable behind a skyline farmstead at the Wardlow crossroads. Was it time to wake Nadin? As if by thought transference, Nadin sat up in his hay, and within the next few seconds was dusting it from his clothing.

They got up and found one of the things they were looking for: a shed where there was a pile of what had once been clothing, heaped on a trestle table. Nadin picked up and threw down again a pair of corduroy breeches, a single canvas gaiter, a coat with the lining protruding from the shoulder. The smell of must and mould was nauseating.

'Now you know why some people say that ours is dirty work,' Nadin said. 'It's reasonable to suppose that he found something here to put on to go to Eyam in.'

Reasonable to suppose: wasn't Nadin being carried along a little too easily by supposition? Nowhere could they find traces of any fire.

'Time we started walking, Tom.'

They set out along the lane which Bagguley must have followed with his load of furniture. By the time they reached a relatively major road, there was light enough for it to be worth Nadin's while to stand still occasionally and survey all points of the compass.

'Imagination, Tom—where can you buy it? To see what Ben Bagguley saw that morning. To think what Bagguley thought. To *be* Ben Bagguley—'

'To be a mental defective,' Brunt said.

'Aye—but a single-minded defective. Bagguley ought in theory to have made things easy for us. And yet—'

He suddenly smote a palm with his fist, pointed to a building in a dip in the road.

'Now why didn't that come into my mind before? Mother Southwell's ale-house—'

It was not a pub in the normal sense of the word: a port of call where ale could be bought and consumed in the back kitchen.

'Ben Bagguley wouldn't be able to bring himself to pass Mother Southwell's, would he? After the night before, his every morning's first drink must be a dire necessity. It's a bit early for us to be knocking her up. And I know these old biddies: they don't remember. When they see how badly you want to know, they make an even better job of not remembering. But we'll not go by in too much of a hurry.'

Very shortly after that, they were in front of Mother Southwell's front door, and Mother Southwell's grey-white curtains were still drawn, upstairs and down. Nadin stood where Bagguley would have halted his cart and looked back up the road they had come along.

'Now what would he have seen, Tom? *Be* Ben Bagguley. What would he have seen that morning to make him late in Eyam?'

Brunt was without notion what Nadin was getting at. It was as if Nadin's new dynamism had dried up his abilities.

'He saw his wife,' Nadin almost shouted, so that Brunt looked up at Mother Southwell's windows, expecting her night-bonneted head to be thrust out in complaint. 'He saw his wife coming back over that brow. And he was not to know about the carrier's back axle. He simply thought she was deceiving him—that she had never meant to go to Chapel-en-le-Frith at all. She had tricked him. She was coming back as she had threatened, to talk to PC Judson—to get ready to turn Queen's evidence, and clear herself.'

'Possible,' Brunt said.

'Inescapable. One idea at a time in Bagguley's head is as much as he can handle. Therein lies the danger of the man—and the simplicity of handling him. And look—that's the way that he would take—'

He pointed to a swell of hillside between themselves and Starve-Acre. It was scarred by the long line of what the locals called a *rake*: a stretching hollow of debris and subsidences where, a couple of centuries before, there had been open-cast mining for a surface lead seam. It would be admirable cover for a man wanting to make a concealed approach: especially a man who knew every stone as intimately as Ben Bagguley did. A length of the *rake* ran over his own land.

'He'd have done it quicker by road in his cart.'

'And all Litton village would have known that he'd been back. Tommy Lamp-oil would have seen him.'

'So what did he do with his horse and cart? He'd not dare leave them here on the road.'

Nadin thought, necessity compelling his brain to find the facts.

'There's a disused quarry a quarter of a mile along the road. Come on, Tom!'

From barrel-organ monkey, Nadin seemed to have become a schoolboy.

The quarry was an overgrown gash in the landscape, the hacking-place of a small farmer who used to burn his own lime. It was set back a little from the road and provided a space in which a small cart could be put out of sight for an hour or so. Nadin's excitement was beginning to approach the comic. He found a little heap of dried horse-manure, showed Brunt a chewing of the bark of twigs, where the horse could have been tied up to a tree. But who was to say whose horse?

Then Brunt made the discovery that mattered—and that convinced him for the first time that Nadin was really making sense. He found the ashes of a fire—a fire that had not gone on burning very thoroughly after it had been left: and that for obvious and disgusting reasons. The yoke and sleeves of a jacket; one charred leg of a pair of trousers; a scrap of the recognizable hessian that had been the sack in which Bagguley had carried the filthy bundle as far as here.

There was something of the schoolboy in Brunt now, too: but Nadin was busy. He was stooping over the horse-muck, picking it up in lumps and throwing them willy-nilly into the distant grasses.

'Get hold of a few loose stones, Tom, and hide that fire. I don't think that that bugger Pickford will have the wits to look in here—but we'll make sure that he finds nothing.'

'But those ashes could save Ludlam.'

'Amelia's going to do that.'

Then they were on the road again.

By the time that Nadin and Brunt had reached Middleton Dale, George Ludlam was being wakened in his cell to face the decisive day. Even his escort seemed to know that this morning he was to be put into the box, to rescue or condemn himself. It was surprising how many people down the line seemed to be in optimistic sympathy with him. He had made a sympathetic impression on men who were normally cynical about their charges. When he was finally ushered up the steps into the dock, his guards were too well disciplined to wish him luck. But he caught the feeling.

Wilfred Hearnshaw was, comparatively speaking, an aristocrat of Ben Bagguley's profession. Jimmy Nadin had had dealings with him in the past over suspicion of holding goods in transit which, in fact, the dealer had had the sense to get rid of. Honours in the warfare between the two had so far been fairly equal: three times Hearnshaw had let Nadin know that he had refused purchases that would have been too dangerous for words. And Nadin had repaid by now and then letting him know that there were goods about which a wise man would not handle. The two men knew the pattern of each other's lives, although not always the details of each other's dispositions. They had both achieved coups—and both had survived.

Hearnshaw shaved twice as often as Bagguley—sometimes as frequently as three times a week. He was the first to wear some of the clothes that he put on, and he could rise on occasion to observances of protocol which Bagguley would have considered soft-centred.

One of these was to offer the policemen breakfast in his own home. Brunt might have considered this prejudicial to their inquiry, but Nadin was not for letting the opportunity slide. Policemen who have done a creditable day's work before breakfast-time have worked up an appetite. And Hearnshaw saw no reason to pass up on the chance of a second session at the board himself. Over his fourth cup of tea, Nadin finally let slip that he would like to see the load of Eva Hargreaves's possessions that Bagguley had sold him.

'That's if it's not already disposed of.'

'Oh, no—it had occurred to me—in all the circumstances—that—'

'Very wise of you, Wilfred. And it would be clever of you to keep the collection intact, in case it has to be returned at short notice to its original owner.'

'I should be heavily out of pocket on that, Mr Nadin.'

'As a matter of fact, I dare say you wouldn't,' Nadin told him. 'There's an interested party who's likely to make good compensation.'

He picked up a chamberpot that had a hole below viable level, due to the snapping off of its handle.

'Where was this lifted from, Wilfred? Chatsworth?'

'Oh, you know how it goes, Mr Nadin. I have to take the rough with the smooth.'

Nadin looked round the barn, stacked rafter-high with decrepitude.

'Where do you keep the smooth, then, Wilfred? And while we're here—just what time was it when Ben Bagguley turned up with his last cargo?'

'You know how it is, Mr Nadin—I'm not a man who's forever looking at my watch.'

'Especially when Ben's already told you what time you must say. Oh, I know you art-dealers have to stick together—'

'It wasn't that, Mr Nadin. Ben didn't want his wife to know about another call he was making.'

Then Hearnshaw saw the concentration in Nadin's eye.

'His wife, Mr Nadin—oh God, no!—I hadn't put two and two together like that.'

'Inspector Pickford, now—he accepted half past ten?'

'Honestly, Mr Nadin—'

'He can't have pressed you very hard,' Nadin said.

'He's a man who believes what other men say. He's not like some I could name.'

'I think Inspector Pickford is likely to be here again, Wilfred.'

'Oh Christ, no!'

'In fact, he's probably on his way at this moment.'

'I'll have to tell him that I made a mistake.'

'You'll tell him nothing of the bloody sort. You'll stick to your story.'

'Yes—but—'

'Or you'll have him preferring charges. Like making a statement, knowing it to be false. Like obstructing him in the course of his duty. Inspector Pickford, Wilfred, is not a man who likes making a second start from the beginning—and having to write out a report saying that he was taken in by the likes of you.'

'Mr Nadin—I only—'

'Well, only do something else. Stick to what you first said. Tell my friend Mr Pickford that you have nothing to change in your statement. Stick to your guns, and you'll make Pickford a happy man. Because if you don't—'

Nadin picked up a ewer, adorned by a device in green, blue and gold dragons.

'If you don't, Wilfred—I do happen to know where this came from. And so did you when you bought it. Because it was on a list that I circulated three months ago.'

Wilfred Hearnshaw was silent for some while. But then his better nature stabbed him.

'But Mr Nadin—if I read my paper correctly—this man Ludlam—'

'Take it from me: that man Ludlam's chances are not going to be affected by your statement. And you wouldn't have given him a second thought if we hadn't called, would you?'

'It's not fair to say that, Mr Nadin.'

'It's bloody true, though, isn't it?'

'You know me, Mr Nadin. All I ask is a quiet life.'

'In that case, why not opt for an honest one? Well, you don't have to take tips from me if you don't want to. But I wouldn't go rocking Pickford's boat, if I were you.'

CHAPTER 21

George Ludlam was sworn, and throughout the court bottoms readjusted themselves to benches. Mr Hartwell began conducting his client through the biographical details that had led him to return to the High Peak.

'I suppose we must resign ourselves to a three-volume novel, the judge said, after the first ten minutes of it had established its pace and density.'

'M'lud, it is important that there should be no misunder-
standing of the accused's mind and outlook.'

'Yes, Mr Hartwell—we are listening.'

Nadin hired wheels to get them back out of Eyam: unresilient
iron wheels, and springs that were no longer capable of their
proper function.

They did not complete their journey into Litton. When
they were within sight of the *rake*, Nadin sent the equipage
back to Eyam. He and Brunt took pains to follow the trail
with the same cunning hillcraft as Bagguley would have
shown—clinging to the hollows, running at a crouch
whenever a short stretch of skyline could not be avoided.

'Yes—he could have done it, Tom.'

They did not go to Starve-Acre. Three hundred yards
short of the farm, they took a wide detour that brought them
into the village through the fields at the back of PC Judson's
house. There they established that Pickford had arrived in
Litton very late last night, that he had spent a long time in
the Cordwainers' Arms, but that he had not stayed the night
there. There had been a persistent lack of spare beds in the
inns of Litton, and he had had to retire to the George at
Tideswell. This morning he had been seen coming through
Litton again in a hired carriage. But this time he did not stop.
He continued as fast as the hills would allow in the north-
easterly direction in which Eyam lay. He must have passed
along the road as Brunt and Nadin were losing themselves
among the scars and pock-marks of the *rake*.

Ben Bagguley had also come back into the village this
morning at about eight o'clock. He had conversed with no
one, except to make a vain attempt to be served with liquor at
the Red Lion; he did not try again at the Cordwainers', but
carried on towards his home, swearing blackly. According to
all reports, he was wearing the thunderous look of a man in
deep-dyed alcoholic aftermath: but that could hardly be
called news. His clothes bore the appearance of a man who

had slept rough in them. But men had often slept rough in Ben Bagguley's clothes before they came into his possession.

Nadin and Brunt went openly over to the Cordwainers', where two of Litton's more inquisitive souls were already drinking in the bar. Annie Barker took the policemen into her kitchen, where Eva Hargreaves was looking surprisingly lively over a bowl of bread and milk. And Amelia Pilkington was looking anything but entranced by the day's prospects. Nadin asked at once about Pickford's visit, and was reassured.

'I kept out of it, as you told me to,' Amelia said. 'Annie put me away in an attic that I'll swear no one else could find. God, what a house this is for getting lost in! I had a job even finding my way back to the main stairs after I'd heard Pickford go. And yet Annie's voice had carried all the way up there, setting up every firework in hell for him for making her disturb a sick old woman at that hour of night. And needless to say, Eva gave him nothing.'

Eva Hargreaves grinned toothlessly over her bowl. However much or little she had understood of it, she had enjoyed the encounter. And she was enjoying every minute of this. It was not lost on her that she was the key to getting the better of a man who had in his way slung as much power about as Needham ever had.

'And now—'

There was a look of unaccustomed fatigue about Amelia Pilkington. No human machine was unexpendable. Amelia merely managed to live most of the time giving the impression that hers was.

'And now—surely you've got enough to go on? I'm not certain what it is you want me to do today. But I think I've got the general idea—and I don't much care for the colour of it.'

'Tom and I will be on hand. We'll be fielding very close in.'

'In the same room, I hope. Jimmy—this isn't going to

work. It didn't work when Pickford tried it on George Ludlam, did it?'

'That was crass,' Nadin said. 'That was Pickford giving a public demonstration of how little he knows about men. Does he think that men like George Ludlam believe in ghosts? Didn't he know that Ludlam would see through it the moment that paint-splashed man-woman came into the room? If you wanted a single statement of Pickford's general state of competence—'

'It wasn't a question of a ghost, Jimmy—you know it wasn't. It was a question of giving him a shock. And isn't that just what you're thinking of doing to Bagguley?'

'Not the same,' Nadin said. 'Never lose sight of human nature. This trick will only work with a man who has something on his conscience.'

'So are you going to have the breadknife lying ready on the table, so that when he comes for me with it, you'll know exactly how he went for his wife?'

'Now that's something that Tom and I hadn't thought of. Annie—can you lend us a knife?'

'If I am to understand your contention correctly,' the judge said, 'the prisoner had no further affection for this Mrs Hargreaves—and had had no such affection for approximately fifty years. And yet he was putting himself to a great deal of trouble on her behalf. I fear you are losing us in all this subtlety, Mr Hartwell.'

'There is such a thing as a compelling nostalgia, m'lud. Also a long memory for injustice and harsh treatment.'

His lordship grunted.

Nadin got Amelia, still threatening to withdraw from the whole farrago, to put on a variety of old rags that Annie Barker had raked together from somewhere. It was not too difficult to create an impression that might work at a distance. A black ensemble, grease and an obscenity of stains were the only fashion-notes that had to be striven for. Amelia Pilkington was pretty much of a height with Molly Bagguley, and with a shawl low over her brow and its corner pulled down over her mouth, she could probably get away with the illusion down to about forty yards.

'But am I supposed to open my mouth? The moment I do that, I give everything away. I have picked up a few Derbyshire words, but a voice is a voice—'

'We are dealing with Ben Bagguley,' Nadin said, 'not a philologist. He was talking to his wife in a drunken stupor last night. She's probably his companion in every drunken stupor that he has. You'll come as no surprise to him.'

She laughed emptily.

'If I can get away with this, maybe I'll try a season of working the workhouses.'

And as they were almost ready to leave the inn, she had another line of second thought.

'And all this for the sake of a man I've never met in my life. Amelia Pilkington—your next address is going to be the asylum.'

'Just you wait till you do meet him,' Annie Barker said, and rolled across the room to plant a kiss on Amelia's cheek. 'Not forgetting that he'll have a lot to be grateful to you for.'

'There you are, Amelia,' Nadin said. 'Annie's conceding him to you. The best stakes you ever played for.'

Mr Hartwell wound up his examination-in-chief at a nicely judged moment for the judge to announce the lunch-hour adjournment. It was not possible to tell from the faces of the jury what effect George Ludlam had had on them. They must surely not be less than fascinated. There must have been moments when they began to wonder about the relevance of the 1820s. But could they resist that display of decency, probity, sobriety and quiet thoughtfulness?

It was this afternoon, Mr Hartwell knew, that a few different angles were likely to be twisted out of the structure.

This afternoon he would learn how big a risk he had taken by producing his client on oath. This afternoon, Mr Broome would be on his feet—Mr Broome, who had been on his backside all the morning, letting the jury see how bored he was by this recital of industrial history.

Carter Broome, QC, was no fool. There were weaknesses in George Ludlam that he would not have missed.

It all depended on what Pickford was going to discover on his second look.

Pickford was let into the Chief Constable's office at about the hour when the court was rising for the judge's afternoon entry.

'I have spoken to the old woman again, sir—and there is not a physician in the land who would declare her admissible before any court. She is inarticulate. She is incapable of continuous thought. She cannot differentiate between the personalities about her.'

Inspector Pickford was hungry and tired—but, to be fair to him, he had put up with hunger and fatigue in some of Her Majesty's outposts. He also understood that a man's outward appearance was all that one's adversaries saw of one. He was wearing a new and elaborate stock, and his boots bore such a polish that the Chief Constable was grateful that his own were out of sight under his desk.

'You will, of course, be submitting all this precisely in writing,' the Chief Constable said.

'Of course, sir.'

'And this alibi at Eyam? I take it—?'

'It is watertight. The man Hearnshaw is a rough diamond, but I will lay my career and reputation on the open table that he is telling the truth in this instance. There was even a telling little point about his watch. It is a watch that Hearnshaw had once offered to sell to Bagguley. Hearnshaw is quite childishly proud of its accuracy. He always made a point of looking at it with something of a flourish whenever

Bagguley called on him. So he can say that it was at twenty-seven minutes after ten that Bagguley arrived at Eyam—far too early for him possibly to have killed his wife.'

'Then counsel for Ludlam's defence can only rely on his power to evoke sympathy,' the Chief Constable said. 'Now—if we might have a word about the future of this man Brunt—'

'I used to consider him a promising youngster. I fear he has been utterly ruined by Nadin, as far as any career prospects are concerned.'

Brunt was under the shadow of a drystone wall that divided fields on Starve-Acre's south-western approach. It was the sort of wall that one could easily associate with Bagguley—its coping gone in places, gaps that had not been made good for years, rubble strewn where cattled had lunged. It made Brunt's task of concealed movement more difficult. There were stretches where his only hope was to crawl. And he had to do this at the speed at which he knew Amelia Pilkington would be walking.

Somewhere behind a wall on the other boundary, Nadin would also be moving forward with caution. Brunt pictured him unnaturally doubled, leaping from cover to cover with the agility he had once seen in a menagerie baboon.

In the middle, following a field path, Amelia Pilkington was walking unhurriedly. Brunt caught sight of her as he hared past one of his gaps, her long black skirts caught by the light breeze, so that the rags were moulded against her limbs in front, and fluttering behind her displaying the heels of her disreputable boots. She was taking advantage of the wind to keep a corner of her shawl blown across her face.

She had continued to have bouts of reluctance. All this came very near to self-sacrifice, she had said, and any of her friends who knew that she was displaying nobility of soul would think that she was losing her grip.

Nadin did not remind her of their original bargain in

Darley Dale. All that seemed an æon ago. She must know
that it had no validity now—if it had ever had. Nadin was no
longer in a position to bring charges based on Reginald
Burdell. All he could rely on was his ability to keep things
moving, hoping that that would hypnotize her to stay in line.

Was it worth the risk and effort? What did Nadin really
expect Bagguley to do? His most likely reaction was a
ferocious physical attack on the woman; and what would
that prove? Brunt examined the terrain, judging the
obstacles that he might have to surmount at speed if the
attack was impetuous. Here the remains of a stranded wire
fence, there the corner walls of a collapsed barn; at one point
a wall dipping down to the middle of a dewpond: if dew bore
any relationship to the green liquid filth that Bagguley had
not scoured out for years.

Brunt leaped ahead in advance of Amelia, plunged down
to lie behind wall-ruins and look back at her. She was coming
on at the same leisurely pace, plucking a blown fold of skirt
away from one knee. She was advancing from the middle of
the field, in full view of the front windows of the house. Brunt
crept forward to a vantage-point.

Nothing seemed to be happening in the house. The farm
had a lifeless appearance, heightened by the stolidity of the
stone and the square, unsymmetrically placed, skittishly
curtained windows. Of the litter that lay about the surrounds, nothing seemed to be in usable order: milk-churns so
rusty that the first attempt to move them would separate
body from base; a cold frame sprouting nettles. Amelia was
only ten yards now from the yard gate. Brunt looked for a
way of circumventing the dewpond. Nadin was not in evidence. There was no telling whether he had managed to stay
abreast of them. Then Brunt was certain that a shape had
moved in one of the upstairs windows—of the room that the
Bagguleys had given to Eva Hargreaves. Had that some
significance? Did it mean that since he had murdered his
wife, Bagguley had abandoned the marital bedroom? If so,

what that a key to his present frame of mind? How had he spent the morning? Had he come home so eroded by yesterday's excesses that he would be physically capable of nothing?

The shape at the window resolved itself into the torso of a man. And then it withdrew, leaving only the blank panes, one of them broken and replaced by a square of weatherbeaten cardboard. Amelia was pushing her body round the wicket-gate, which was broken and would not open properly.

Mr Broome actually smiled at George Ludlam.

'Your evidence has been a mass of unclear insinuations. In this court, of course, we are in no way concerned with hearsay—and yet this morning we seem to have heard very little else. I would like to establish, Ludlam, whether you honestly believed the rumours that a family in Litton had had something to do with advancing the deaths of certain old people?'

'I neither believed them nor disbelieved them.'

'But you wanted to discover whether they were true or not? How did you set about that?'

'I asked questions of possible witnesses.'

'And did you prove anything?'

'I *proved* nothing.'

'But you were keenly interested?'

'Of course. It was rumoured that yet another person was in danger—someone with whom I had shared grievous experiences a long time ago.'

'So if you had managed to prove anything, what would you have done about it?

'I don't know. My inquiries had not gone far enough.'

'You would not have gone to the police?'

'Probably not. It seemed to me—it still does seem to me—that the police had been nearer to events than I could ever be—and had done nothing about them.'

'Let us have a clear single answer: you would not have gone to the police?'

'I might—I might not. On balance, I think not.'

'You are most anxious to impress us with your honesty, Ludlam?'

'I have no need to do that. I am under oath.'

'Putting it in somewhat threadbare terms—you would have taken the law into your own hands?'

'I do not know what I would have done.'

'But it would have been some form of independent action—Ludlam versus the Bagguleys?'

'You could put it like that—since it means nothing.'

'I *am* putting it like that. That is what is implied in the charge with which you stand arraigned. Would you call yourself a man of equable temperament?'

'Usually.'

'Would you care to expand that?'

'I mean that I can be provoked—and that provocation is cumulative.'

'Those are big words, Ludlam. Do you mean that you have occasional outbursts of anger?'

'Occasionally.'

'How occasionally?'

'I have lost my temper about six times in the whole of my life, I think.'

'And do you feel one of those occasions creeping up on you at the moment?' Broome asked him.

'I see no reason why it should.'

'Not if I remind you that one of the six outbursts of your life took place in Starve-Acre farmhouse, the last time you confronted Mrs Bagguley?'

'It would have been pointless, considering the state I found her in,' Ludlam said.

CHAPTER 22

Brunt knew that Bagguley would only have left the window for one reason—to come lumbering down the stairs. The distance between Amelia Pilkington and the door was diminishing. At any moment now, Bagguley would be opening that door. Brunt did not know where Nadin had got to, or how much he had seen. He moved down to the edge of the dewpond.

And Bagguley did open the door. He was turkey-faced and wild-eyed. In his hand he held a kitchen knife. From a pocket of his jacket protruded the neck of a bottle, so that the dominating impression was one of degeneracy rather than aggression.

Then Amelia did a brave thing. She said afterwards that it was because it occurred to her that he had picked the knife up for defence rather than attack—he was afraid of what he saw coming through the gate. She stretched out her arms, so that the wind sent a train of garments streaming behind her. And she screamed—a shriek that would have done credit to an actor on Tod Slaughter's boards.

The folds of her shawl had only to drop from her face, and Bagguley must surely know. Or would he? As Nadin had once said—one can see only so far into an unreasonable mind. How far could one hope to penetrate into Bagguley's? Who could tell how far he was from seeing the monsters of *delirium tremens*?

Amelia held out her arms and approached within three yards of him. Brunt caught sight of Nadin coming up on her left into what had, years ago, under different management, been a vegetable-garden of a sort. Bagguley dropped his knife and bolted, up the side of the farmhouse, across the yard, heading for where the first scar of the rake dipped into a

furrow on the crest. Nadin was after him, Amelia falling
back, Brunt slipping on the edge of the pond and discovering
that its filth was even worse than it looked. It seemed as if
half the village was now stumbling behind them across the
field: Judson had appeared, Billy Orgill, Peter Townley—

Bagguley turned his head and saw the pursuit, and Amelia
Pilkington raised her fluttering arms again. Bagguley turned
and faced the mob, his lungs bursting from an effort that he
was in no condition to make.

'Keep her away from me!'

His hand went to the bottle in his pocket.

'And, Don't!' Nadin shouted to him. 'It's a terrible death,
Bagguley. You saw what Isaac Slack went through.'

Bagguley was trying to get a grip on the cork. Nadin threw
a stone from close quarters. The glass shattered and Bagguley howled as the undiluted acid coursed down his fingers.
Amelia came within a yard of him, her arms flapping like the
wings of an angel of death.

'Keep her away from me!'

It was not an articulate confession—but there were a dozen
men on hand to hear the froth of self-incrimination which
effervesced from Bagguley's lips until Nadin promised to
restrain the woman in black.

And in any case, the charred clothes in the quarry, though
hidden, had not been destroyed. And Wilfred Hearnshaw,
though bewildered, carried more conviction when he was
telling the truth than when he was inventing lies about his
watch.

Mr Broome sat down well satisfied that he had left nothing
undone to destroy the impudent image of integrity in which
Hartwell had dared to clothe Ludlam this morning. Hartwell
would not have cared to be seen looking at his watch, but he
knew roughly what time it was. His lordship would surely
not want the closing speeches to start this afternoon.

Ever since they had returned from lunch, Mr Hartwell had been hoping to see the solicitor's clerk slip into court with the folded note that would announce the watershed of the proceedings. It had not happened, and the barrister therefore believed now in his heart that there could not remain much hope for his client. That was not to say that there was none at all—but Mr Hartwell knew that he would need an hour or two alone this evening before he could think of any.

The reason why the solicitor's clerk was delayed was because Nadin still had to get from Litton to Derby. And even this was easier to achieve than gaining direct access to the Chief Constable. It was only because the Chief acutely associated Nadin with the High Peak and Pickford that he agreed to see him as rapidly and unconstitutionally as he did. He listened closely, did not need to have anything explained to him a second time—and did not ask any questions that would have confused the issue.

'By the way, Sergeant Nadin—you are leaving us next week, I believe?'

'That is so, sir.'

'Can you give me an honest opinion of this young man Brunt? Have you succeeded in teaching him anything, do you think?'

CHAPTER 23

On the 2.45 out of Miller's Dale, Amelia Pilkington and George Ludlam were travelling first class. It was a luxury that they had debated. After the hurly-burly of the past few weeks, neither of them really wanted to rub shoulders with the common mob.

In a cloud of smoke and steam they were engulfed in the tunnel that cuts off all view of the Litton Mill. Amelia laid her hand on Ludlam's shoulder.

'I shall thank God when we're out of this county. And let all this be a lesson to you, George. Forget the past. Don't look back over your shoulder, not ever again.'

'I couldn't resist it, Amelia. They were bad days at Needham's.'

'Then let them stay half forgotten. While you were getting mixed up with the Bagguleys, I was facing it alone in Buxton and Darley Dale.'

'Well, thank God you didn't trip up. Or else—'

They passed the gap between the two tunnels. Ludlam had been on the watch for it, and stood up so as not to miss the crags and waters of the dale.

'And I had such a lovely one lined up for you in Matlock Bath. A mining engineer who cleared up a fortune on the Rand, and is now very happily married—with correspondence from two Afrikaaner women that he'd buy back at any price.'

'Sorry, George. Nothing else in this part of the world.'

It was a Manchester to London train and it was not scheduled to stop at the Derby suburban station Nottingham Road. When it did show signs of pulling up, Amelia and Ludlam thought no more than that they were slowing down for the main Midland Road station. They paid no attention to what was going on on the platform, did not see two men looking in at window after window, were aware of nothing special until Brunt and Nadin got in and sat down close on either side of them.

'Nice to see that you two have got together at last,' Nadin said.

'Yes. We've enjoyed getting to know each other,' Ludlam answered.

And he looked at Amelia with pertinent affection.

'Who can tell what will become of it?'

'Who cares what becomes of it, as long as it doesn't happen in this beautiful county?' Nadin told him.

'I don't quite see what you mean by that.'

The train was in motion again now, creeping slowly into Midland Road.

'I mean anything you care to make of it.'

The train stopped. There was a lot of bustle, and a delay of some minutes while the engine was changed. Nadin did not speak again until there was no danger of newcomers to the compartment.

'Quite an adventure, wasn't it?' he said then.

'Not one I'd care to repeat,' Ludlam said.

Nadin turned to Amelia.

'You'll just have to take greater care of him, won't you?'

She smiled sweetly, and looked at Ludlam coyly.

'I'm afraid that that's something that I can't anticipate yet.'

Nadin pointed to something through the window—a river at the far side of a meadow.

'That,' he said portentously, 'is the Trent.'

They looked as if that had little meaning for them.

'In less than a minute we shall cross that mighty stream. And then we shall be in Leicestershire. Which will make me a happy man—because it will mean that you two have passed out of the county that I love. Another thirty-six hours, and it will not be my concern. But a man called Pickford, in a moment of pomposity, has submitted his resignation. Never a wise move to make, because there is always the chance—as has happened, much to Pickford's surprise—that it will be accepted. But young Tom will be staying at his post. I can only trust that you two will remember how well he knows you.'

Nadin and Brunt alighted at Loughborough. It was obvious, really, Nadin had told Brunt. A good deal of the story that Ludlam had told about himself had been true—Needham's mill, his escape from there, his journey with the wandering trades unionists, the lives and styles of Billy Orgill, Eva Hargreaves and others. He had indeed made a name for himself as a master worker in wrought-iron in the provinces and free cities of the Germanic Confederation.

But by the 1860s the palmy days were beginning to fade. The industrial revolution had come later to Central Europe than it had to Great Britain, but it had brought with it, as Ludlam had said, a preference for mass production. Ludlam had spent some months without a commission, until he managed to win a small order for renovations in a few of the ornate rococo churches of the south.

When he had completed this, working his way through Baden and Württemberg, he had stopped off at Baden-Baden. Here—at first for his own amusement—he had observed the machinations of a young Englishwoman who was living on the fringes of expatriate society. She was not doing anything very exciting—begging for her fare home, weeping for doctor's fees for an aged aunt or a dying sister. She was keeping body and soul together, managing to pay her way in the only hotels worth staying at, but that was about all.

The possibilities appealed to George Ludlam. He did not care for wealth and idleness—particularly not for English wealth and idleness. He knew of too many Englishmen who had lived on the labours of the Pancras children and others. Things had got better now, but even now he saw too many drawing the lion's share from spinning frames and weaving sheds.

These people resting their gouty joints and repairing their abused digestions in Wiesbaden, Bad Wimpfen and Bad Harzburg—they were the very ones who could afford to keep him and Amelia in that state of comfort to which they would be glad to accustom themselves.

He played a game with Amelia, pretended to catch her *en flagrant délit*—then suggested that with his high degree of sophistication and knowledge of the world, he was the very one to move ahead of her, finding targets for her talents. She became very fond of him, and they worked their way down the Rhine Valley, across into the fashionable Channel coast resorts—until finally curiosity and nostalgia brought them back home.

But on that London train there was something not entirely friendly about Ludlam. He ignored Brunt and Nadin as they waved from the Loughborough platform.

But Amelia waved back happily enough. And as she did she silently mouthed the words, 'Le Touquet.'